THE VOICE OF LITTLE WOLF

"And what will you tell the White Man, Little Wolf?"

"I will tell him that our people were raised far up in the North among the pines and mountains. That in that country we were always healthy. That there was no sickness and very few of us died. Now since we have been in this country we are dying every day. This is not a good country for us and we wish to return to our home in the mountains . . . If you are going to send your soldiers after us, I wish that you would first let us get a little distance away. Then if you want a fight we will fight you and we can make the ground bloody at that place."

THE BRASS COMMAND

The BRASS COMMAND

Clay Fisher

BANTAM BOOKS

TORONTO • NEW YORK • LONDON • SYDNEY • AUCKLAND

THE BRASS COMMAND
*A Bantam Book / published by arrangement with
the author*

PRINTING HISTORY
Houghton Mifflin edition published May 1956
Bantam edition / September 1971
2nd printing . . . . . June 1972   3rd printing . . . January 1980
4th printing . . . September 1988

HISTORICAL NOTE

THE BRASS COMMAND is a work of fiction. It does not pretend to be history.

Nevertheless, its story is told against a factual military background, and for that reason certain of the principal characters, notably the responsible white officers at Fort Robinson, Nebraska, have been provided with names, ranks and serial numbers which never existed.

Others, such as famed General George Crook and the leading subchiefs of the Powder River Cheyenne—Little Wolf, Lone Crow, Left Hand—are drawn from life; as are Red Cloud, White Thunder and Three Bears of the Sioux. Dull Knife, the tragic patriarch of the Cheyennes, is fashioned from material furnished by surviving tribal historians, some of whom were small children at the time of the terrible retreat. The same sources have supplied the picture of "Little Red Bird," the old chief's legendary twelve-year-old grandson.

Neither irrefutable proof nor unchallengeable fact is herein claimed. The following account is but one student-observer's circumstantial reconstruction of a sanguinary case of Indian crime and white punishment which occurred seventy-five years ago on a lonely army outpost in northwest Nebraska.

C.F.

Tongue River Reservation,
Lame Deer, Montana, 1954

CHAPTER 1

SHORTLY AFTER 6 P.M. that crisp fall evening of September 1, Colonel James McAllister left the officers' mess at Fort Robinson, Nebraska, complaining of sudden nausea and a slight pain in his lower right side.

By midnight, both pain and nausea had become intense and Surgeon R. L. Cummings had diagnosed the condition as "a severe green colic." Subsequently, he prescribed an anodyne of camphorated tincture of opium, issued an irritated prognosis of complete recovery by morning, stomped back across the parade ground cursing his calling and wishing he had bucked for his commission in any branch of the service but medicine.

Cummings was as good a reason as existed why the army called its medics surgeons rather than doctors. Or, by any stretch of the definition, diagnosticians. By 4 A.M. Colonel McAllister was in an agony of abdominal cramps. Sometime before dawn his appendix burst. High fever, delirium and terminal coma succeeded one another in the swift course of the peritonitis and he was dead with nightfall of the 2nd.

The command at Robinson, spottily staffed as were so many in the far western posts, passed down through three temporarily vacant grades of rank to First Lieutenant J. T. Jackson. Undismayed, the young officer, a cool man with a long eye for the opportunities of rapid advancement inherent to combat commands in the Indian country, took over. It was typical of him that he did not notify Department of the Platte Headquarters at Fort Laramie of McAllister's death until the morning of the 3rd, calmly taking the disordered evening of the 2nd to host his new staff at a formal mess and to indoctrinate its uneasy members with the fact that until orders to the contrary might be in official receipt John Tenney Jackson was the Lieutenant Commanding at Fort Robinson, Nebraska.

It was further in line with his character that he quite confidently expected headquarters to confirm him in the post. He was presently up for his permanent captaincy, had to his prior credit two years of combat service under both Crook and Mackenzie. In addition, he knew Crook personally, assumed that the old warhorse of the Platte would remember him.

In the latter assumption he was correct.

Crook remembered him.

By return telegraph, over the signature of Captain John G. Bourke, Crook's Acting Assistant A.G. at Laramie, came the information that a Captain H. K. Weston had been ordered out from Lincoln to assume the Robinson command. Weston would travel by rail as far as Sidney Barracks, 125 miles to the south. He would arrive there the 7th, report to his new post at Robinson no later than the 9th, take over with the temporary rank of major.

Possibly as a sop to Jackson for having been passed over, but far more likely as an unrelated coincidence, the same message carried confirmation of the latter's overdue promotion. The new captain and acting C.O. at Fort Robinson had at most five days in command remaining. He made the best or, depending upon the viewpoint, the worst of them.

As McAllister lay dying in his lonely northwestern fortress death was also striking far to the south.

At Fort Reno near Darlington, Oklahoma Territory, three gaunt Cheyenne chiefs crouched in a smokestained cowhide tipi and watched soundlessly as the weary smile on the face of a fourth Cheyenne faltered, faded, went finally vacant. Iron Mountain, the forty-first of Dull Knife's tribesmen to set forth upon the long ride into the Land of the Shadows since the band's arrival at Fort Reno the previous year, was dead.

Little Wolf stood up.

He pointed his pipe to the four cardinal points of Mother Earth, south, east, north and west, blew a slow drift of the smoke toward the opening in the lodge's peak and toward Maheo, the Cheyenne All Mighty. "It is done," was all he said. "Bring the shield."

He spoke to the first of his companions, Little Chief. The latter arose, went quickly toward the rear of the lodge and the tripod of willow poles upon which rested the bullhide circle of Iron Mountain's war shield. Removing the shield, he bent and placed it upon the dead chief's breast. Then, carefully scooping from the tipi's dirt floor a small handful of *hesec,* the blessed

2

mother soil, he mounded it gently upon the center of the shield and began the guttural intonations of the Cheyenne Death Song. Outside the lodge, Iron Mountain's womenfolk caught the first notes of the lament. They began to sway upon their haunches and to croon, in minor key accompaniment to Little Chief, the eerie cadences of the chant. There was no other outcry.

Within the lodge again, Little Chief's incantations ceased as abruptly as they had begun. The third and last of the death watchers came to his feet. "Who will be the next?" asked Dull Knife of his companions. "It is *Tono'ishi*, September, the Month of the Cool Moon. Yet the fever remains and it will not go away and our people die a little more each day. How long must we wait, my brothers?"

"No longer," said Little Wolf, his lean hand reaching for his Winchester.

"It is truly a bad thing," muttered Little Chief. "I am an old man and I have seen nothing like it since the Big Sickness." He referred to the cholera epidemic of 1849 in which over half the Cheyenne Nation had perished but Dull Knife waved the allusion aside.

"This is no cousin to that sickness," he said. "We would not die now if we were well at heart. It is not our people's bodies which die here but their spirits."

"We will wait no longer," repeated Little Wolf grimly. "We will go home now."

"Yes," agreed Little Chief slowly, "let us go to Miles now and tell him."

He spoke of John D. Miles, Indian Bureau Agent for the Darlington Reservation, a respected friend of the Cheyenne and a man in whose fairness each of the northern nomads had a savage's trusting faith. Still, any decision of the Cheyenne to inform their agent they were actually leaving the reservation was a tremendous one. The very simplicity of Little Chief's suggestion that they now do so, struck the chill of that decision's meaning into both his listeners.

It had been little over a year since they had voluntarily come in to General Crook at Fort Robinson and been sent in subsequent treachery to the humid plains of central Oklahoma. In that year the twin plagues of dysentery and malaria, against which the mountain-bred northerners had no natural immunity, had decimated their tiny band. On a starvation diet of rotten beef, weeviled flour and maggoty fatback their people

3

had sickened and died like quarantined cattle in the inescapable wallow of their own filth.

Now, ravaged alike by hunger and disease, with only a few muzzle-loading rifles, less than two days' hoarded food supplies and a miserable remuda of grass-thin ponies, the question had been called on a march of eight-hundred miles across an alien territory of three states and four army departments; a friendless land which twenty-four hours after their departure into it would be swarming with aroused white settlers and pursuing cavalry troops.

The decision, finally, was Dull Knife's. He made it with the same simple dignity Little Chief had shown in proposing it. "Aye," he nodded quietly, "let us go to Miles and tell him we are going home."

"Yes!" Little Wolf warned them with sudden vehemence, *"and this time we will do it!* Do not forget that, my brothers."

The way he said it and the way he looked at them when he had said it gave the two older chiefs pause. Dull Knife was the tribal head of all the Northern Cheyenne. Little Chief was the revered keeper of their sacred medicine arrows. But Little Wolf was their War Chief. He was the dedicated Dog Soldier, the undisputed leader in battle and upon the trail. When he spoke like that and when he looked like that, older and more thoughtful men grew slow with their questions.

"And what will you tell Miles?" asked Dull Knife, looking straight at him. "How will you say it when we are really there in front of him?"

In return, Little Wolf's voice grew softly bitter. "I will tell him," he said, "that our people were raised far up in the North among the pines and mountains. That in that country we were always healthy. That there was no sickness and very few of us died. Now since we have been in this country we are dying every day. This is not a good country for us and we wish to return to our home in the mountains. This is what I will tell him."

"And you, my brother?" Dull Knife nodded to Little Chief.

"I," said the older man, "will tell him that a great many of us have been sick. Many have died. I myself have been sick a great deal of the time since I have been down here in this hot southland, homesick and heartsick and sick in every way. I have been thinking of my native country and the good home I had up there where I was never hungry. But where, when I wanted something to eat, I could go out and hunt the buffalo.

4

It makes me feel sick to think about that and I cannot help thinking about it. In this way will Little Chief tell it to Miles."

It was good and fair talk but Dull Knife was still watching Little Wolf. "And so, Hokom-xaaxceta," he used the Cheyenne familiar diminutive name, "what will you then say when you have said this to Miles and he has told you *no?*"

For a long time Little Wolf was silent. But when he spoke there was more of sadness than anger remaining in his deep voice. "When Miles has said no to me," he began, "I will take his hand in mine, using my left hand because that is the side my heart is on. Then I will say to him, 'My friend, I am going now to my camp. I do not wish the ground about this agency to be made bloody but now listen to what I have to say to you. I am going to leave here. I am going back north to my own country. I do not want to see blood spilled about this agency. If you are going to send your soldiers after me, I wish that you would first let me get a little distance away. Then if you want a fight I will fight you and we can make the ground bloody at that place.'"

He paused, putting his slim hand on Dull Knife's bowed shoulder. "Do you understand me, my father? Do you see what is in my heart and what it is that I will do when I have said this to Miles?"

It was Dull Knife's turn to hold the long silence and to let it grow. He drew four times upon his dying pipe before his stooped shoulders straightened and the dark light of his pride-in-race and of his chieftainship of such as Little Wolf showed brightly and for a last moment in his old eyes.

"I understand you, my son. Let us go to Miles." Then, with the sign of the pipe made swiftly toward the open smokehole of the lodge, *"May Maheo watch over us."*

CHAPTER 2

"Does it strike you," said Sergeant Meeker, pulling in his horse, "that this here particular seventh of September sees us concluding an assignment of considerable distinction?" The lean-faced little cavalryman was not talking to his horse but to a mounted companion, a surpassingly homely giant astride a tall bay gelding.

"It does," conceded Sergeant Lundy, checking his own mount and waving the halt back to the eight troopers and the mule-drawn field ambulance which the latter escorted. "It does, and for the past 123 miles I've been pondering how best we might repay the dear captain for the privilege."

"Consider our position," nodded Meeker. "Yonder lies the lovely village of Sidney Barracks. Yonder," he pointed to the field ambulance, "lies the 'honored shell' of our late commander, all furbelowed with the blessed regimental guidon and—"

"And *hell*," interrupted Lundy. "Yonder we got the god-forsakenest collection of board-and-batten shacks this side of Huachuca, Arizona. And yonder we got poor old Colonel McAllister in a pine box with a lousy Third Cavalry flag tacked on one end and a four-bit piece of stars-and-stripes bunting snagged around the other. Some 'honored shell' mister."

His companion looked at him. John Henry Lundy was a six and one-half foot, slow-minded, hill country Oklahoman of mixed white and Cherokee blood. He was a behemoth of a man with the moral fortitude, as he himself put it, "of a wet mouse." Still, like Meeker, he was a twenty-year regular. When he got that dumb scowl of his to working like he had it working now, it was time to hold up and inquire what might have his rear-end in the air.

"All right, Johnny," Meeker asked quietly, "what's eating you?"

"Sam," the big sergeant's nod was one of sober concern, not bad temper, "it's this new C.O. we're supposed to pick up in Sidney—Westburn, or Whetstone, or whatever the hell his name is. Hang it all, we put a colonel we're certain of aboard a baggage car for Omaha. Then we pull a major we don't know nothing about off a daycoach for Robinson. Down where I come from we don't cotton to them kind of blind swaps."

Meeker eyed him "To a bat," he observed caustically, "there ain't no other damn animal can see nothing either."

"Come off the big talk," challenged Lundy bluntly. "What the hell you mean?"

"I mean I know a little something about this here new major. We done met professionally."

6

"Since when, by cripes? You ain't never said nothing about it before."

"Well now, when I was with Crook over in the Big Horns—"

"We've heard all that. What kind of an officer is this here Wenstrom?"

"You simmer off for five seconds, I aim to tell you. He was on Crook's staff at the time, taking a tour of field duty from some desk job back east. Naturally, he stayed behind when the General sent Mackenzie and the rest of us in after Dull Knife's village. Ah brother! That was a wild night. Snow to the horses' bellies. The mercury turned blue and froze in the bulb at thirty-five below. Them Cheyenne women screaming. Them slanted-eyed little Injun kids—"

"Damn the Cheyenne!" snapped Lundy angrily. "So you was one of the heroes that slaughtered them poor devils in 'seventy-six. I asked you what kind of an officer this new major was."

"And I just told you, you mulehead. He's a *staff* officer. A real nice, quiet little gentleman."

"Sweet Jesus!" growled the giant Oklahoman, *"a little gentleman!* Just what we need at Robinson right now, ain't it? What with upwards of eight thousand horse Injuns squatting between us and the agency up to Pine Ridge!"

"Don't surrender to the Sioux just yet," advised Meeker thoughtfully. "This here new C.O. may still have one qualification for the job. At least one that Captain Jackson sure as hell ain't."

"Such as what?" demanded his companion belligerently.

"Such as he might like Injuns," said the other sergeant quietly.

Lundy nodded. He knew exactly what Meeker had in mind. If there was one officer on the western frontier best suited by a dangerous combination of cavalry pride and Indian contempt to raise four kinds of red hell around Fort Robinson, that officer was Captain John Tenney Jackson. "Well," he said at last, "providing he does, I reckon we might yet get through to spring with our hair all in one piece."

The Union Pacific's train No. 6, westbound out of Omaha and waypoints southeast along the Missouri, pulled into the Sidney Barracks siding at 8 P.M. Watching her chuff up through the fall darkness, Lundy slid down from his perch on an empty baggage truck, flipped his cornshuck cigarette away, grunted uninterestedly, "Yonder she comes, Sam."

Meeker, aroused from his back-flat position on the same vehicle, eased down to the station platform, knocked the dottle out of his cob pipe, straightened his blouse, spat unenthusiastically into the rising wind. "Yeah," he said, and, having said it let it go at that.

Neither man felt moved to larger observation. As for Meeker, the new major was an already known quantity. As for Lundy, Meeker's description of the latter had contained the two lowest definitions in the combat soldiers dictionary, "staff officer" and "gentleman."

Sight unseen, big John Lundy had written off Fort Robinson's replacement commander. Going now through the dusk toward the slowing train to meet him, the hillman's jaw set up like rim ice around a January waterhole. Moments later, peering into the smoky light of the coaches' lamps at the slender figure alighting from Car 3, that rim ice broke away under the spread of a catfish grin wide and warm enough to thaw a hole through a six-foot snowbank.

"Lord love us!" gasped Sergeant Lundy, *"it's little Hollie Weston—"*

Having gasped it, he stood and stared as joyously dumb-struck as though the Union Pacific's train No. 6 had just delivered the second coming of the Saviour upon the windswept boards of Sidney Barracks' lonely station.

Lundy's glad cry of recognition was seconded by the snapping of a full brace into what had started out a grudging half salute. "God bless you, sir, I never in the world expected to see *you!*"

"You never expected to see me make major anyway, eh Lundy?" The slim officer's reply was backed by a wry smile but there was nothing cynical in the way he reached for the big sergeant's hand.

"No sir," objected the latter, "that ain't it at all, *Major!* It's just that it's been such a power of time since last we shook."

"It sure has, John." The quick smile faded. "I suppose I should have made brigadier by now but you know how it is."

"Yes sir," blurted Lundy unthinkingly. "It's a mighty long haul *without the ring.*" He saw the twitch of the muscles run the corners of Weston's mouth, hit awkwardly back into his brace to cover his embarrassment. Weston shook his head. "As you were, soldier. Don't go regulation on me. Who's your small friend?"

8

Meeker stepped forward, saluting and answering properly for himself. "First Sergeant S. B. Meeker, sir. G. Troop, Third Cavalry." Weston nodded. "Glad to know you, Meeker. You two boys the full committee sent over to welcome the new brass?"

"No, we ain't," Lundy broke in. "We got a squad along. Brung Colonel McAllister's body over in a field ambulance. Wagon's to go back full of Springfield fodder. Captain Jackson's orders. We're in for trouble, likely."

"Trouble?"

"Injun variety," said Lundy without elaboration.

Weston's eyes narrowed. "I thought the Sioux had quieted down after Crook rounded up Dull Knife's band and sent them south last year."

Lundy wagged his head, his broad face troubled. "That's just it. Them damn Cheyenne—"

"Go on."

"Well now it's only Injun talk, Major. I allow I wouldn't pay it no particular heed, providing I was you."

"Which you're not."

"Yes sir." Lundy shifted his feet uncomfortably. "Well, the Sioux they're saying the Cheyenne are coming back to Robinson. That they ain't going to stay down there in Oklahoma much longer and that they'll start north before the first snow falls. Colonel McAllister, God rest his good soul, he always took proper stock in Injun talk. But Captain Jackson he don't pay it hardly no mind at all."

"I'm not worried about Captain Jackson," clipped Weston. "What about Sergeant Lundy?" He knew from their earlier association that the big Oklahoman had had a fullblood Indian mother, been born and brought up in the old Cherokee Nation. He watched him now with resultant closeness.

"Me," muttered Lundy, "I always allowed that it took Injun blood to smell Injun blood."

"And you're smelling it in this Sioux talk about the Cheyennes coming home, is that it?"

"Till I cain't get the stink of it out of my nose, Major. And I'm only *half* Injun."

Weston watched him a moment longer, then shrugged.

"All right, let's go." Lundy saluted, relieved. "Yes sir. Me and Meeker will get your things. You'll be wanting to spend the night here at the barracks."

"I'll be wanting," corrected Weston, "to borrow Sergeant

Meeker's horse. Meeker, you collect my duffel and bring it along in the ambulance tomorrow."

Lundy's heavy brows went up in disbelief. "Our horses are a mite tired, *sir*."

"So am I, *Sergeant*." There was no mistaking the soft return of the emphasis. Lundy took the hint in his stumpy teeth, ground down hard on it. "Yes sir, we'll get the horses," he gritted.

"Thanks." Weston's peculiar smile was back again. "I'll be right here on this baggage truck." He was stretched full length and half asleep before the two sergeants had cleared the station platform. Looking back over his shoulder, Meeker muttered thoughtfully. "Now there's a cool bird. Maybe I sighted him in a little short."

"You did," agreed Lundy. "Him and me was boot corporals in the old Fifth."

"Boots, for the luvva Pete? How'd he get his bars?"

"Field brevet, by God." Lundy's blue eyes were sober with the memory of it. "The Rebs had five troops of us in a bad bottle in them cussed woods just outside Appomattox. Every one of our officers was dead or down. This skinny Weston kid took over and fought us clean through Longstreet's whole brigade. We busted out on Sheridan's flank and so help me little Phil himself give Weston the brevet then and there."

A sudden thought and not a comforting one, took Sergeant Meeker. "Lord Almighty," he breathed softly, "ain't Captain Jackson going to love that!"

Lundy did not have to ask him what he meant. Captain J. T. Jackson was a rank-conscious, Academy-ring West Pointer; the kind of professional career officer who recognized no lower form of military life than the commissioned enlisted man. "Yeah," he finally answered Meeker, "likely him and Major Weston will get on cozy as two bull elk in October."

"Any chance of laying a month's pay on the winner?" queried the other sergeant hopefully.

"All depends, Sam. Which bull you want?"

"Which you think? The Captain, naturally."

His hulking companion nodded stupidly, broke into his vacant, guileless grin. "Well, mister, you've got yourself a bet. And I ain't even going to ask to examine your teeth."

"What in the name of hell," demanded Sergeant Meeker, at once suspicious, "are you talking about?"

10

"My old daddy," alleged Sergeant Lundy, straightfaced, "always told me never to look no gift horse in the mouth."

CHAPTER 3

CAPTAIN JACKSON was quite a cavalryman. He fancied himself to rank somewhere beyond Crook and close to Custer in native genius. He studiously patterned his dress and mannerisms after the latter. Which was to say he affected the wide black Stetson, soft-tanned kneeboots, red silk neckerchief and fringed elbow gauntlets of the late "boy general," and that when he addressed the red brother in formal council at the Fort Robinson officers' mess, as he was doing the evening of September 8, he conducted himself with an abrasive mixture of fighting cocksureness and sarcastic courtesy.

"I have been hearing," he directed his remarks to a tall, hard-faced Sioux who sat first on his left at table, "too much of this talk about the Cheyenne coming home. But I have not been hearing it from you. May I suggest that it is not the way of chiefs to whisper outside the lodge and to carry tales about the camp like squaws?"

The choice of the word was as unfortunate as it was deliberate. Red Cloud came to his feet, dark eyes glittering. His long arm swept dramatically down the line of his brother chiefs, his voice deep with emotion as he recalled his people's finest hour in the Custer fight. "Here sits White Thunder!" he rasped. "He was first in the fighting which cut Reno away from Yellow Hair. Next to him I see Three Bears. He led the braves who kept Benteen away from the river. Beyond them are Young Man Afraid, Rocky Bear and Sorrel Horse; past them, Six Feathers, Black Coal and Sharp Nose, our Arapaho cousins. All were there that day along with Greasy Grass. All fought like chiefs." He paused, swinging his proud gaze back upon Jackson, throwing his arms wide in oratorical appeal. "Do you now say that they are squaws!" he demanded fiercely.

It was Jackson's turn to find his feet. He did so awkwardly.

11

There was no misreading the defiance in the famous Sioux's challenge. Nor the scowling silence with which his fellow chiefs approved it. The young officer flushed, his reply coming with the uncertain quickness of defensive bad judgment.

"I am saying that it is the way of women to whisper a thing behind the hand. If that is not your way, you have only to speak out. I demand to know what this nonsense is that you are spreading among your people. I mean these lies about the Cheyenne coming back here to Fort Robinson!"

So far the exchange had been conducted in the formal phrases of the Dakota dialect, Jackson being one of perhaps a dozen army men on the frontier who had a speaking command of the guttural Oglala tongue. Now, Three Bears, the implacable white hater, sprang to his feet. He struck his chest, crying out in thick, halting English, "Me Mato Yamani, Three Bears! Me no lie!" The others down the table struck their chests in turn, grunting the Sioux courage-word *"H'g'un, h'g'un!"* to show they understood the insult and agreed with Three Bears's angry exception to it.

But Red Cloud had been to Washington upon the iron horse. He had been the guest of the Grandfather and had looked upon the white man's mighty cannon and vast armies. He realized far before his less traveled brothers the hopelessness of his people's position. "Enough," he now counseled them wearily, "let that be an end to it." Then, softly, to the waiting officer, "You have called us liars and women. We have listened. Now we will talk."

"Ha-ho, thank you!" Jackson's bow was a study in faultless elaborateness. "It is most gracious of you!"

The Sioux chief did not recognize the mockery by so much as an eyelid flicker. Impassively, he waited for the white officer to have done with his youthful foolishness. Then, quietly, he translated for him the sounds of the south wind among his lodges.

All year long, he told Jackson, the word of his people had traveled north upon that same wind with disquieting news. The Cheyenne were dying like deer flies in the hot, humid climate of the Oklahoma plains. There was but one doctor for five thousand Indians down there. There was never enough food and what there was, was poor and bad.

Now, suddenly, a more ominous word was coming north. Dull Knife and Little Wolf had had enough. The Cut Arm

People would come home now, back to the Big Horns and the Powder River and the *He Sapa,* the sacred Black Hills.

That was the new word which came to the Sioux at Pine Ridge Agency. If the army wished to cover its ears and Captain Jackson chose to call it lies, Red Cloud could not help that. But if the Cheyenne came back there would be trouble. Among Red Cloud's lodges were many who remembered the death of Tashunka Witko, the great Crazy Horse, and who still blamed the treacherous surrender of the Cheyenne for it. If Dull Knife's people now returned to Fort Robinson, Red Cloud could not say what the Sioux might do.

When he had finished, the Oglala chief sat down. Now it had been said. Now it was up to the white officer. Red Cloud had warned him, no man could do more.

Jackson took the little minute of following silence to think —or to do what passed for thinking in his shallow opinion of Indian threats, implied or actual.

He knew that Dull Knife, fleeing Crook and seeking sanctuary with Crazy Horse in the winter of '76 following Mackenzie's destruction of the Cheyenne village, had been refused asylum by the Sioux chief. In angry retaliation Dull Knife had sought out Crook and surrendered his entire tribe to him at Fort Robinson early in '77, thus hastening and in effect forcing Crazy Horse to surrender his own fierce Oglala. Upon that surrender, the haughty Sioux, resenting his white guards laying rough hands upon his person, had struggled with the soldiers and been fatally bayoneted through both kidneys.

Knowing all this and having himself been actual party to much of it, Jackson still missed Red Cloud's point. "If you are afraid of the Cheyenne," he snapped at the tall Oglala, "let me assure you that I am not!"

"I am not afraid of the Cheyenne," explained Red Cloud patiently, "I am afraid of the Sioux."

Even with the point repeated, Jackson refused to acknowledge it. "Nonsense! You show your fear of them in every word and movement. But let me lend you a little of my own courage." He leaned forward, shifting into English and striking the palm of one hand with the balled fist of the other to emphasize his points.

"The Cheyenne will never break away from Fort Reno and the soldiers down there. Should they try, they would not get one march away from the agency. If they did, they would

13

have between them and their precious Powder River three military departments of the United States Army, and should they by any fantastic stretch of the imagination succeed in crossing those departments, they would never dare come back here to Fort Robinson but would scatter up the Platte somewhere beyond Laramie and toward the Big Horns.

"Now then," he concluded, straightening to stand at arrogant parade dress, "do you quite understand all that?"

Red Cloud and the other chiefs looked at him. They looked at one another. They all shrugged, all looked speculatively back at the white officer.

"We understand it," said Red Cloud quietly.

"Well then, what do you now say?" The Captain, secure in his final command of the situation, lapsed graciously back into the Oglala dialect. Red Cloud stood up. Each of the other chiefs came noiselessly to his feet behind him. "We say," grunted their leader, "that the Cheyenne *will* break away from the soldiers down there, that they *will* march across your three army lands, and that they *will* come back here to Fort Robinson."

Having said it, Makhpiya Luta, the Red Cloud of the Oglala Sioux, followed by the proud file of his fellow chiefs, turned his back upon Captain John Tenney Jackson and stalked out of the Fort Robinson officers' mess.

Ordinarily it was a decent two days by horse, four by wagon from Sidney Barracks to Fort Robinson. Weston pushed eighteen miles in the remaining hours of the 7th, halted only when midnight, failing horseflesh and an isolated ranchhouse arrived in timely conjunction with Lundy's grateful groan that even a first sergeant could sit a McClellan saddle just so long. The big soldier's relief lasted long enough for Weston to get the rancher up and swap him out of his two best cow ponies. Within twenty minutes they were remounted and moving out. An hour after the stop they were another ten miles down the military wagon-road. Twenty-three hours and two brief rests later the shaggy little range horses were stumbling, heads down and hocks wobbling, toward the main gates of Fort Robinson.

During the last mile down the long grade east of the post Lundy, unable to keep his military place another minute, blurted out an injured demand to know "what the hell the big rush was all about."

14

"My orders, Sergeant," Weston brusquely informed him. "I was to report at Fort Robinson on the 9th. It will be the 9th in exactly eleven minutes. I'll be there."

"Thank you, sir," Lundy grunted. "A man don't mind killing two horses so long as he knows it's a matter of life and death."

Weston deliberately ignored the caustic flippancy. It was any worthwhile N.C.O.'s privilege to gripe, any halfway knowing C.O.'s wisdom to let him get away with it. He knew Lundy, Lundy knew him. They understood one another. So, at least, thought Major Howell K. Weston.

But with the main-gate sentries countersigned and falling behind and with the naked-board elegance of the Bachelor Officers Quarters looming ahead, Sergeant Lundy was in something less than heartfelt agreement. He was, in fact, angrily scowling over his recent delight at seeing Weston climb down off that daycoach at Sidney Barracks. Clearly, cursed the burly Oklahoman to himself, Fort Robinson's new C.O. was a powerful lot closer to Meeker's disdainful "staff officer and gentleman" than he was to Lundy's fondly remembered "little Hollie Weston."

The joys of that September 9th's early hours were not yet complete for Sergeant Lundy. Nor for any other enlisted or commissioned man then suffering assignment to Fort Robinson, Nebraska.

At 5 A.M. the key in the post telegrapher's shack broke into a nervous chatter. At 5.01 young Corporal Peter Feeney reached sleepily for his message pad. At 5.02 telegrapher Feeney forgot all about being sleepy.

Shortly after 5.03 he was waving his message under the nose of Captain Jackson's orderly and advising him that "he damn better well roust out the C.O., if he didn't want his stripes ripped off and shoved where he'd have hell's own time finding them without a flash lantern."

"Listen, Feeney," objected his fellow corporal, "pipe down will you? I've got my future to think of. Besides, get in line and wait your proper turn. I got another billy-doo for the late Captain Commanding that come in ahead of yours."

"The late what?" demanded Feeney scowlingly.

"You heard me, soldier. The new C.O. is here. Checked in over at the BOQ four hours ago. Sent orders along not to bother Captain Jackson till morning."

"Mister!" spluttered Feeney, suddenly remembering what he held in his hand, "Captain Jackson's going to be bothered no matter what orders the new C.O. sent along. Read this."

Jackson's orderly took one look at the message, handed it back like it was a hot stovelid. "God Amighty!" he gasped. "I'll get the Captain up, you take this on over to Major Weston."

"She's on her way," grinned Feeney. "Give my love to the 'late' C.O.!"

Regardless of Fenney's parting smirk, or the other corporal's replying curse, the message still said what it said, and despite Captain Jackson's subsequent ugly surprise and Major Weston's swiftly following shock, it meant what it said. As of the 3 A.M. blackness of that September 9th, 1878, Dull Knife's Northern Cheyenne had broken away from Fort Reno, Oklahoma, and the Darlington Agency, and were presently outward bound for their Powder River hunting grounds.

Their quietly announced primary objective and last major encampment on the long march home?

Emomoxae, brother. Very simple.

The Niobrara Sand Hills and Fort Robinson, Nebraska!

CHAPTER 4

IT WAS NOT YET 5.20 when Captain Jackson came across the parade ground. First light had barely begun to streak a little cold gray along the ridgepoles of the post's lonely scatter of buildings. Still, as he walked, shoulders braced, back yardstick straight, the Captain was taking a troubled, farewell look at his brief command.

In 1878 Robinson was not a fort in the sense of earlier outposts like Laramie, Kearney and C. F. Smith. There was no stockade, no old-fashioned fire towers, no lookout catwalks, no log-buttressed rifle slits. There were only the board-and-batten sprawlings of a base camp's workaday structures—the troop barracks, company kitchens, mess halls, hospital, machine and blacksmith shops, sutler's store, supply depot, saw-

16

mill, stock barns and cavalry stables. Beyond these, there were the empty hayricks and cattle corrals dating from the year before when Robinson had been the beef issue point for the abandoned Red Cloud Agency. After them, there was nothing but the reaching emptiness of the prairie wastelands.

But with all its loneliness Fort Robinson was an important command, one wherein a young and forceful administrator might come in contact with both general officers of considerable service weight and junketing congressmen and senators of important influence with the War Department, and one wherein a man of Captain Jackson's remarkable energy might easily make a great deal of military hay, given a few weeks of clear weather to get his crop in. The fact he had been granted but five days in this ripe field before being replaced by an unknown staff officer from the East was turning in the youthful cavalryman like a rusted Spencer bayonet as he hesitated just outside the officers' mess.

The pale lamplight from within the building did little to soften either the misery of that last moment, or the harsh lines it brought to his face. Still, the pause was strategic, not nostalgic.

Major Weston was in the mess ahead of him. His orderly had dutifully warned him of that. Furthermore, he and Weston had never met, though both had been with Crook in '76. Captain Jackson was a man who well understood the values of military first appearances before one's new commanding officer. Accordingly, he re-squared his shoulders, shook off his unhappy scowl, stepped quickly toward the door. Seconds later, in the little grace note of time supplied by his superior's failure to notice his entrance immediately, his concern over his own appearance was suspended in his surprise at Weston's.

He saw a man of advancing middle age, forty-five at least, he thought. Only moderately tall, he was of slender, almost girlish physique. His face was bone-thin, his closely cropped hair a startling snow white. He was plainly, from the distracted way he sat over his coffee cup staring into space and drumming the tabletop with his slim fingers, a man of undetermined, nervous disposition.

Altogether, Captain Jackson was very pleased with his quick appraisal of Major Weston. He was much less than he had expected, or feared. He appeared to be precisely what post rumor had said he was: a staff officer and "barracks brigadier" of no combat background. A man, in effect, who would be forced and no doubt glad to turn over the active duties of his new post to his aggressive, more experienced second-in-command.

Howell Weston took more time with his look at the youthful captain.

Glancing around with what the latter interpreted as an uneasy start, he nodded soberly, motioned the youngster to join him. Jackson returned the nod, moved stiffly across the room.

Studying him, Weston saw a very blond young man of perhaps twenty-five or six. He was strikingly handsome, powerfully set up. His deeply tanned face was distinguished by a wide, firm jaw, good mouth, clear hazel eyes and a lustrous, fine-flowing Custer mustache of superb sweep and dash. He was presently booted, spurred, big-hatted and ready to ride as though the Cheyenne were five miles from Fort Robinson rather than fifteen from Fort Reno.

Weston liked what he saw.

The boy was a shade young and no doubt a little cold-jawed and of a mind to fling his head under curb. But he was every inch of his six feet the professional combat soldier and hard-riding frontier cavalryman. Right now, faced in his first chance at field command with an Indian outbreak which figured to wind up squarely in his own inexperienced lap, Major Weston was indeed glad to get up and offer his hand to Captain John Tenney Jackson.

The first hint Jackson got that the new C.O. might not be quite as distracted as he had assumed was the small map the latter produced the moment the introductions were done. "I've been doing a little preliminary thinking, Captain." He smiled. "I'd like you to tell me what you think of it." He pushed the map hesitantly across the table. "Naturally, it's only paperwork."

Naturally, Jackson thought, but only said, "Yes, sir, glad to, Major," and picked up the map.

His careless glance narrowed suddenly.

Drawn with lead pencil on the back of Corporal Feeney's message sheet, the sketch revealed in amazing detail parts of seven states and five territories. Commencing with Texas and the Indian Nation on the south and ending with Dakota Territory on the north, it encompassed the entire heartland

18

of the Plains Indian country between the Rocky Mountains and the Missouri River. In itself, this would have been enough. There was more.

Darlington Agency and Fort Reno were accurately marked astride the mid-Canadian in Oklahoma Territory. Fort Robinson was precisely placed beyond the Niobrara in Nebraska's northwest corner. In between, every major stream of the eastern divide drainage was correctly indicated, while across their impeding east-west courses from Reno to Robinson stretched a neatly dotted line showing Weston's calculated assumption of Dull Knife's line of march. Included was a detailed set of marginal notes giving estimated dates and probable distances to be covered by the Indians from day to day, together with a terminal prediction of the time of their arrival among the Sand Hills below Robinson.

From any angle one might choose to look at it, it was a remarkable document.

The hands on the mess-hall clock stood at just 5.23 when Jackson finally nodded and handed the paper back to Weston. That map had been drawn from pure memory. And within the past twenty minutes.

"Well," said Weston interestedly, "what do you think of it?"

There was no doubt in Jackson's mind as to what he thought of it, nor any confusion in it as to being candid on the subject. "It's quite a map, Major," he sparred. He felt like saying, So what the hell of it? but instead forced a smile. "I'm surprised at your grasp of our territory."

He did not say it as though he meant his and Weston's territory. It was the editorial "our," identifying it only with himself. If Weston caught the slip, his answering smile failed to show it. "I'm afraid maps are an occupational hazard of my military background, Jackson. I've never fought a campaign on anything but paper. Back at headquarters they called me Captain Cartography."

"Headquarters, sir?" No further information on Weston had as yet come through channels and Jackson was curious to know more of his new chief's official connections.

"Sheridan's staff. I was up at Lincoln on some minor business for the General when this thing came up. I fear being available, geographically, constituted my main qualification for the job, Captain."

Jackson, drawn past the edge of customary respect by Weston's manner, put his most anxious foot forward. "But

19

why on earth didn't you beg off, sir? After all, a man of your years in service—"

"Exactly, Captain." The quiet smile was gone. "There's the whole point—a man with my years in service."

"Sir?"

"Jackson, when a man has been a professional soldier for nineteen years, the last thirteen of them riding a desk and writing field orders for lieutenants half his age, he doesn't 'beg off' a chance like this."

"I'm afraid I don't follow you," frowned his listener, though he followed him all too well. "What chance do you mean?"

"Let's put it another way," nodded Weston. "When a desk officer has sat thirteen years in grade without a promotion, he doesn't shy away from an opportunity at active field command." He cocked his lean head, eying the younger man closely. "I mean *this* chance, Jackson, exactly as I said."

"Good Lord, sir! Do you actually mean you wanted this godforsaken command? That you really saw any chance for yourself here?" There was the quick flare of resentful anger in the questions; the old, harsh, thoughtless anger of youth railing at age for being in the way. Weston read it clearly in the rising excitement of his companion's voice, yet he only looked away from him, his own voice going softer still.

"When you are as old in the service as I am and have done nothing to distinguish yourself or your profession, you live constantly with the fear of failure. Hours become important, even minutes. Each tick of the clock sounds as relentless as the drip of a leaking canteen. You live with time, every empty second separating you farther and farther from the end-ambition of any man's pride—the final need to prove himself to himself."

He broke off, coming around in his chair to face his junior, gray eyes intent. "Jackson, I feel very strongly that Fort Robinson is the *last* chance for me."

As quickly as it had previously faded, the half-shy smile was back again. "Of course, I'm quite sure General Sheridan felt the same way in suggesting me to General Crook, and that Crook agreed in his reluctant approval. Still, after nearly twenty years I've been given a chance in command. I don't suppose any man your age can appreciate what that means, can he Jackson?"

"Why, yes sir, I think he can, Major!"

Jackson surprised himself with the vehemence of his reflex

20

sympathy. Something in the compelling way the older man had spoken had broken through his tight armor of ambition. There was a quality close to naked loneliness in Weston's words. A helpless candor which made them sound like an outright appeal for support and understanding in a situation for which he had small heart and large incompetence. Jackson was touched—if but for the moment.

"At least *I* can," he went on impulsively. "And I want you to know, sir, that you can count on me."

"Thank you, Captain."

It was all Weston said, yet the way he said it made the younger officer flinch. Jackson was already reconsidering his generosity. Already damning himself for what he considered an inexcusable display of emotion. He tried to think of something to say that would set the record straight, could not find the words, had to wait for Weston to continue.

"Well," nodded the latter, "let's get back to the map and this Cheyenne business." Returned to military ground his voice altered perceptibly. Preoccupied with his own thoughts, Jackson failed to note the change.

"As you will see," Weston went on, "I figure them to take approximately three weeks to reach the Niobrara Sand Hills. That is, providing we have not meanwhile been notified of their apprehension to the south. Naturally, you are more familiar with their abilities to march than am I. Point and question, sir: what do you think of my calculations?"

He asked it with his slow, disarming smile—and trapped Jakson into his first tactical blunder.

Misreading the apparent invitation to do both, he stepped carelessly past the last boundary of relative rank, treated the question with flippant familiarity. "Oh, surely now, Weston, you're not serious!" he laughed.

"About what, Captain?" asked the latter softly.

Jackson, riding over the warning quietness of the question, spurred roughly ahead. "Why, about the Cheyenne of course! They'll never get one mile from Fort Reno, much less within five hundred of the Niobrara."

"I see," said Weston, still soft with it. "Then I understand you to propose we take no unusual precautions here at Robinson?"

"Good Lord, of course not. What on earth would you propose, Major?"

Weston looked at him, then let his glance go back to

21

the vacant corner of the room with which it had seemingly been concerned when the young officer first entered. His slender fingers resumed their distracted drumming of the table-top. At considerable length he nodded slowly to himself, turned thoughtfully back to his waiting junior.

"I would propose, Captain Jackson," he said, *"that you are a damn fool."*

CHAPTER 5

THE FALL NIGHT was dead-still as the whisper of August wind in dry grass. The unshod ponies of the five Cheyenne made no sound as they topped the starlit ridge and came to a hard-breathing halt. Their riders sat them like graven images, black against the leaden sky beyond. While the weary ponies flared their nostrils and lifted tired heads to the smell of the water below, their masters held their silence, peering first into the darkness toward the stream, then back into the gloom whence they had appeared.

Behind them, to the south and east, lay Fort Reno and a fireless, foodless march of forty-eight hours. Before them lay a nameless prairie stream, beyond it, eight hundred miles of open plains and Fort Robinson. It was a time for desperate rest and for a saving of long talk.

"What water is that?" asked Dull Knife of the dark-skinned, scowling chief beside him.

"I am not sure, father," said Little Wolf quickly. "I think it is the Medicine Lodge."

"It will do," ordered Dull Knife. "Red Bird—" He called the name softly into the darkness. The fifth rider, a boy of no more than twelve, moved his shaggy mount forward. "Aye, grandfather. I am here."

"Go back quickly now," said the old chief. "Say that we have found good water and some cottonwoods for the fires. Tell the people to follow you here."

The boy's reply was to wheel his pony and kick him into a laboring gallop back toward the two hundred and fifty women and children and fifty rearguard warriors who composed the main column of the Cheyenne retreat. Watching him go, the old man muttered to Little Wolf. "He is a worthy grandson. He will make a warrior one day."

Little Wolf looked at him sharply, corrected him softly. "He may one day make a worthy grandson. He is already a warrior."

"Aye," sighed Dull Knife. "When the days grow short the years grow long. He should still be hunting rabbits with blunted arrows."

"Late or soon," grunted Little Wolf, "a man will become a man when it is his time." Then, deep voice quickening, "Come, father, let us go down there and scout the water."

"Yes," Bull Hump broke in, "let us go scout the water and light the signal fire."

"We will make it a very small fire," added Wild Hog cautiously. "Just that big to fill a Cheyenne's eye, not one stick bigger."

"Do not worry about the Pony Soldiers," rumbled Little Wolf. "I will watch for them. *Nonotov!* Hurry now. The night is our friend but she will not wait forever."

The frosty hours fell away. Four o'clock and the first streak of the false dawn found Little Wolf still on the ridge, still motionlessly scanning the murk of the prairie to the south. Taking a last look, he turned to the thin warrior who had come up to relieve him. "All right, I will go and get a little sleep now. Watch most carefully when the real light comes. I will be in Tangled Hair's lodge."

Beyond an expressionless nod the young brave gave no sign of his understanding. Nor had he need to. Of all the Cheyenne none had such eyes as his. None could see so far, nor fly so swiftly with the warning when he had seen. The camp was safe with Aeno-anos, the Yellow Hawk, upon the ridge.

For two hours there was nothing but stillness above the sleeping village. Then, with the new sun rimming the graying wastelands to the east, Yellow Hawk's famous eyes grew suddenly fierce with far looking. The next moment he was pushing himself back off the ridge, leaping to his feet and bounding down the slope.

To the scout's excited cry of *"Mila hanska! Mila hanska!"* Little Wolf came upright upon his buffalo robes within Tangled Hair's tipi. The lean chief had no need to delay over the translation of that dread phrase. It was a borrowed Sioux name meaning "long knives," and referred to the issue sabers of the regular U.S. Cavalry. In the present usage it meant the hated Pony Soldiers, and Little Wolf was already pumping the first magazine cartridge into the empty chamber of his Winchester as he sprang out of Tangled Hair's lodge.

"Where? How many? How far?" he snarled at Yellow Hawk. "Say it, you fool! Is your tongue in an otter trap?"

"South!" shouted Yellow Hawk. "There, beyond the ridge. A mile, maybe. No more. Many of them, two hundred at least."

"How are their horses?"

"They look strong. Move fast, at a good trot. Not much dust. They are picking up their feet very clean."

"Bad, bad!" cried Little Wolf. "It will mean a fight."

"No, my son." Dull Knife had come up in time to hear the last of it. "There must be no fight. We will go out and talk to them."

"We will do as *I* say, father." He was gentle with it but Dull Knife and the others who were now hurrying up understood him. Little Wolf was the War Chief. He was taking command.

"I will go out," he promised, his hand going to the old man's shoulder. "I will talk all I can. But there will be a fight if they make one. I will go up on the ridge so that they can see me and send a scout forward to talk to me. I will lift my gun to the sky to let them know we want only to be left in peace."

He broke off to begin barking his orders to Wild Hog and Tangled Hair, and to the eagerly gathering pack of younger warriors behind them. "Do not any of you shoot until the troops have fired. Let them shoot first. Have your guns and horses ready when I go out. If they kill any of us, I will be the first. *Then you can fight!*"

Minutes later he was on the open prairie beyond the ridge listening to Ghost Man, an Arapaho Government scout known to him as an Indian whose word could be trusted.

"Hear me now, Hokom-xaaxceta," pleaded the latter. "These troops are from Fort Elliott over in Texas. They are very young, very nervous, very new out here. The officer with them has never been after Indians before. You had better

24

come on over and talk and for Maheo's sake keep your old people quiet and your young men back on that hill!"

Queried as to the troops' orders, the Arapaho said that he believed the Cheyenne would have to surrender and return to Fort Reno at once. The only promise offered was the old, vague one of better rations and more decent treatment. Little Wolf replied that he would never surrender but that he would come over and talk and maybe something would happen. All the Cheyenne wanted was to be left alone.

"Tell them," he instructed the nervous Arapaho, "that we do not want to fight them but that we will not go back. We are leaving this country. We have no quarrel with anyone. I hold up my gun that I do not wish to fight the whites." With the grave words he kept his promise to Dull Knife, raising his Winchester overhead with both hands in the truce sign. He then concluded abruptly. "But we are going to our old home to stay. Do not try to stop us."

Ghost Man, noting the growing numbers of the Cheyenne warriors along the ridge behind Little Wolf, departed at once across the open ground toward the impatient white commander. As he did, Wild Hog and Tangled Hair were having difficulty keeping their young men in check. Unconscious of the fact, Little Wolf waited alone on the buffalo grass below them.

Presently the white flag went up alongside the regimental guidon and the troop commander edged his horse out of ranks a few steps into the open grassland. Ghost Man accompanied him, waving across to the motionless Cheyenne chief the hand-signs of the truce agreement. Little Wolf returned the graceful signals, started his own pony forward. At the same time his followers, unable longer to sit still, began edging down the hill behind him. They meant only to come to the bottom of the rise, halt there to await the results of the parley. But Ghost Man had spoken with a straight tongue about those white troops from Texas—they were green as the spoiled gall from a sick mountain sheep.

Whether the shots were fired on command as a warning to the moving Cheyenne, or in edgy disobedience through "Indian nerves" will never be known. Whichever the reason, a ragged volley broke from the white ranks as the warriors started down the hill behind Little Wolf, and one of the wild balls tore along the ribs of the War Chief's pony, smashing the wiry mustang to his haunches.

Little Wolf rolled free of him, unhurt. He tried desperately to regain his feet in time. It was too late. The hump-fat was in the fire. *Ghost Man! That Arapaho son of a sneaking camp-bitch! He had betrayed them!* There was an instant yammer of hoarse cries from the enraged Cheyenne. Before their downed leader could recover himself and indicate he was uninjured, his warriors swept past him and on toward the white troops. The firing became general. Within thirty seconds a full-scale "Indian brush" was under way.

When nightfall of that September 11 brought an end to the day-long exchange of reckless red charges and countering trooper volleys, three Pony Soldiers and five Cheyenne had earned their six feet of prairie turf forever. Unsung in death but cold and empty-eyed as any of his three white brothers, Ghost Man, the innocent pawn, lay shot through the heart by Little Wolf himself.

Sometime before dawn of the 12th the Cheyenne struck their lodges and disappeared northward into the rough hill country of the Cimarron badlands. Behind them the time for peace lay hopelessly glazed in the staring eyes of three young Pony Soldiers who would never see Fort Elliott again. Ahead now lay only that other time. That grim, bad time which Dull Knife had so long prayed would not come again to his people.

But it was here now. Not even an old man's rheumy eyes could fail to see it. You peered ahead through the soundless night and your heart grew bad within you. Yet there it was and it would not go away.

Emeoestove, the time of the bull-hide shield and the black charcoal greasepaint.

Emeoestove, the time of war.

CHAPTER 6

It was 10 p.m. of the 13th when Corporal Feeney came on to relieve Private Willy Haggerty in the telegraph shack at Fort Robinson. Ahead of him, he imagined, lay eight good hours of nothing but nodding contentedly over a dead key. Twenty minutes later he was groaning, "Oh, cripes, not again!" and fingering back his acknowledgment of the message from Fort Elliott, Texas.

At 10.05 Major Weston had the bad news and at 10.15 the half-clad members of his staff, clustered around his table in the officers' mess, were getting it, and getting, with it, their first look at his Cheyenne map.

"Here is where it happened, gentlemen." With his stub pencil Weston carefully marked the crossing of the Little Medicine Lodge, while his juniors looked at one another behind his back, palmed their hands in the superior tolerance of youth for dotty old age, did their faintly amused best to pay attention to his continuing, fatherly instructions. "That should put them close to the Cimarron tomorrow. I'd say about here." He made another of the precise pencil notations and Jackson could contain himself no longer.

"Beg pardon, Major. But what difference does it make where they will be tomorrow? Or the next day? They can't get past Fort Dodge and the Arkansas. Colonel Biddle has eight troops of the Seventh there now. Within forty-eight hours the forces from Reno and Elliott will join up behind them and they'll be trapped. They'll never put a set of pony prints beyond the Arkansas. You must know that, sir!"

Weston looked up from his map, the odd twist of his smile flicking his mouth corners. "Is that your considered opinion, Captain Jackson?" he inquired.

"It is," answered the latter tartly, and forgetting to add the customary "sir."

The older man nodded. "Will you please look at the map then, *sir*. Right where I have my pencil."

"Yes *sir*," Jackson amended the oversight, "I'm looking."

"What do you see, Captain?"

"Fort Reno, Oklahoma," said Jackson, flushing under the suddenly interested regard of his fellow juniors.

"Just so. Now then, where am I placing my pencil?"

"On the Little Medicine Lodge River, below the Cimarron."

"Exactly. And how far would you say it was from notation A to notation B. In definite miles if you please."

"I suppose somewhere in the vicinity of a hundred." The young officer's scowl was out in the open now. "Just what's your point, Major Weston?"

"My point, Captain Jackson, is that the Cheyenne are

27

nearly one hundred miles from Fort Reno. Unless memory fails me, it was your previously considered opinion that they would not get one mile from it."

Softly put or otherwise, it was a full-dress rebuke. Jackson knew it. He demonstrated there was more than blunt ambition and rash pride to his character in the way he took it. He shook off his scowl, managed a guilty smile. "Well sir, if we're going to quote from memory you will still have to mark me one-half right."

"How's that, lad?" Weston's paternal friendliness was back on its easy pace.

"I also said they would never get within five hundred miles of the Niobrara, sir." The youngster's returning confidence showed briefly in the hardened set of his smile.

"And—?" Weston question-marked it with inviting gentleness.

"*And they won't!*" Jackson planted his prediction as flat as the sole of a drill sergeant's boot. Sought, belatedly, to soften its fall by widening his stiff grin. And awkwardly shrugging his broad shoulders.

Weston only nodded and turned away from him, speaking quietly to the others. "Captain Jackson is on record, gentlemen. Let us proceed."

They moved forward, bending over the map. As they did, a surprised hint of fresh respect was revealed by the exchange of raised eyebrows among them. Clearly, for all his hesitant manner and apparent humility, Fort Robinson's new C.O. was no fool. At least he was not buying any set smiles, stiff grins or cover-up shoulder shrugs the evening of September 13, 1878.

Within the week, the Cheyenne made a liar out of Captain John Tenney Jackson.

On the fourth day from Fort Reno they reached the Cimarron, halted to water and graze their horses and to rest their women and children. While the lodgepoles were going up, a gray horse troop of the Seventh, quartering down from Fort Dodge in search of them, cut their trail at the Cimarron Crossing. They followed it up swiftly, charged the half-made camp on sight and without reconnoitering its position. Or their own.

It was a hilly, cut-up country, the kind which had always been bad for white troops, and there were no more than twenty minutes of daylight remaining. The clash was brief and bloodless.

This was not the old Seventh of Custer's day but a new outfit of beardless boys and Academy-issue officers. They bore no resemblance to the boot-tough bravos who had followed Yellow Hair into the shallow hills and the oblivion of the Little Big Horn two years before. A regiment of them would have had little business tangling with sixty shield-age Cheyenne. A single troop under a boy lieutenant who had never seen a wild Horse Indian before had no business whatever doing so.

Only the determination of the Cheyenne to at all costs avoid white bloodshed saved the troopers from joining their regimental hero in whatever hunting ground is reserved for no longer active U.S. Cavalrymen. They were allowed one charge through the disordered scatter of lodgepoles, unpacked cowskins, cursing squaws and yelping children. In the wild course of this brave dash they injured four camp kettles, three lodgeskins, a village cur and an old packhorse. After that, it was Little Wolf's turn.

As always when on a war march his braves had their picked night horses tethered alongside each lodge site. Before the gray horse troop could re-form for the rush back through the camp or even get their mounts slowed to begin thinking about that rush, the Cheyenne were running up on their startled tails. The young lieutenant, learning fast, showed promise of some future as an Indian fighter. Without hesitation he waved his bold troops onward—in the same direction they were then galloping—as far and fast and straight away from the screaming Cheyenne as clumsy government horseflesh could take them.

Little Wolf did not linger to savor his triumph.

That troop could have been an advance partol for Maheo knew how many other Pony Soldiers. Also green replacements or not, the Cheyenne remembered that red and white guidon with the big 7 in its center. The lodgepoles were repacked at once and with full darkness the village was again on the march northward.

Forty-eight hours and ninety miles later, another sunset came swiftly down.

Peering into its western cloudbank the wizened Little Chief grew suddenly uneasy. He told Dull Knife to forbid the squaws to unpack the lodgepoles just yet, warned Little Wolf to keep his warriors mounted and the line of march unbroken. He, Little Chief, would first need to make a smoke and consult the Medicine Arrows about this place. He had a feeling they would tell him it was a bad place to camp.

In his pagan way, the Cheyenne medicine man predicted better than he knew.

To the west of the halted column ran the small stream beside which Dull Knife had planned to pitch the lodges. North, two miles, lay the broad ribbon of the main Arkansas. Both east and west of the proposed campsite, flanking it much too closely, rose a series of prairie ridges high and long enough to hide any number of the enemy.

Which was exactly what those ridges were doing at the moment Little Chief's heathen instincts compelled him to load his pipe and keep his people mounted. Mounted behind their silent crests, tensely waiting for the tired Indians to break column and begin setting up their lodges, were four troops of regular cavalry—160 men, eight sergeants, four lieutenants, two captains and a full chicken colonel from nearby Fort Dodge.

But Maheo had not forgotten his people.

The troops had no Indian scouts along, did not correctly read the slow ceremony being conducted by the old charlatan with the buffalo-skull headdress and the long stone pipe, thought it must be some customary blessing of the campsite and waited, accordingly, for it to be done and for the Cheyenne ranks to break apart.

They waited in vain.

Little Chief's smoke smelled bad to him and suddenly, without apparent signal or decision, the Indian column was moving on a high lope up the valley toward the Arkansas. The Colonel stood in his stirrups with an inspired bellow to the bugler. The stirring notes of the charge bit shrilly into the evening quiet. The close-packed troops swept down upon the rear of the Cheyenne march.

It was too late in the afternoon.

No white troops, superior force of numbers to the contrary, ever whipped a band of High Plains Horse Indians in a running fight. The present action proved no exception to the frontier rule. The Cheyenne cut away from the main trail, raced for the cover of the opposite eastern series of ridges, got their women and children and old people safely behind them, turned and struck back viciously at the leading troops.

The soldiers were driven back and fell into a disorganized mill on the open ground of the trail. With their surprised hands full of howling, wheeling warriors on both flanks and with the fire from the hidden rifles of the squaws and old men on the ridge above beginning to get into their front, they soon broke for the shelter of their own, western ridges.

In ten minutes the sun was down, the shooting over.

But for the Cheyenne, only the shooting.

No fires could be lighted, no shelter set up. They had a twelve-hour grace of darkness in which to rest themselves and dry-graze their horses. There was little water left, the buffalo paunch-skin waterbags having been largely exhausted on the long flight from the Cimarron. Only a few pounds of fly-blown agency beef remained, less than two ounces for each of the old ones, the women and small children. The warriors and the boys past ten ate nothing, drank only the cold night-wind.

The scouts went out shortly before midnight to investigate a stain of nightfires against the sky to the north. They were back within the hour. The news was bad, all bad.

Up there, between them and the Arkansas Crossing, was a big camp of white civilians from Fort Dodge out to support the troops in defense of their settlement. Their bonfires stretched along the prairie for half a mile. There were many wagons, and saddled ponies were tethered in picket lines, four deep, beyond the wagons. *Nohetto,* it was a real bad thing.

"*Ai-ee,* Hokom-xaaxceta?" they asked hopelessly of Little Wolf. "What is to be done?"

What was to be done was very little, and exceedingly desperate. Little Wolf knew that. Their ponies would not stand another long nightmarch to swing around the blockade. They had traveled a hundred miles the past two days under heavy carry and without water. The way was bitter but it was clear.

"There is but one thing to be done now, my brothers," he said at last. "You all know what that is." He turned to Dull Knife. "Tell them that I speak the truth, father."

"Aye, my son." The old man's words were heavy with the meaning of the War Chief's request. "I had prayed this time would not come again. If we kill a soldier who is trying to kill us, they call it war and think little of it. But if we kill a settler who is trying to kill us, they call it murder and will

31

hang us for it. Still, you are right, Hokom-xaaxceta. We must do it. It is either that, or surrender and go back."

"*I will never go back!*" With the savage cry Little Wolf glared at the other members of the circle. "You speak for me, Hokom-xaaxceta," grunted the slow spoken Tangled Hair. "And me!" snarled Bull Hump in restless second. "I will count the first coup!" boasted Wild Hog, striking his chest. "I will kill them like cattle!"

"Maheo will bless us," gestured Little Chief, waving the doeskin case of the sacred pipe in finality. "Let it now be done as Hokom-xaaxceta has said."

It *was* done in Little Wolf's way. With the first streak of dawn the Cheyenne charged the wagon camp at the crossing, killing one civilian and wounding eight others. The settlers fled across the shallow Arkansas. The Indians did not pursue them. They wanted only a little time and water. They got both before the Dodge civilians could rally, or the colonel get his sleepy troops up to the scene of the shooting.

All that seventh day they fought a slow retreat up the south bank of the Arkansas, their object to get west of Fort Dodge for their crossing. Because he knew reinforcements would be on their way from the fort the colonel had his troops keep the action at long range. No further casualties were taken on either side. Nightfall found the embattled Cheyenne where they wanted to be—safely west of the white man's big garrison at Dodge City.

The colonel, expecting them to try an early dawn crossing, put his troops across the Arkansas in the covering darkness, had them in position by daylight to enfilade any Cheyenne attempt to ford the river. He quite confidently expected a slaughter. But Little Wolf was a light sleeper.

During the night his scouts had ridden ten miles west and discovered a genuine manifestation of Little Chief's faith in old Maheo—an isolated camp of white buffalo hunters. These latter were to all appearances unaware that there might be a hostile horseman within a month's march of the Arkansas. With first light they discovered that there was. At the same time, the good colonel from Fort Dodge cursed in his carefully trimmed U. S. Grant beard, while he stared across the river at a Cheyenne campsite as lonely of red life as a crater on the far side of *Tono'ishi,* the autumn moon.

That buffalo camp contained eighteen freshly killed cows,

thirty fine examples of Christian Sharps' latest rifles, three packmule loads of modern, brass-cased ammunition. It also contained seven veteran white hunters who were as Indian-dusty behind their hairy ears as the pursuing cavalry were damp behind theirs.

Those hunters also understood the guttural Cheyenne tongue.

When Little Wolf barked at them that none would be harmed who cared at once to set out on foot across the "Milky River," not a man among them chose to argue the old camp creed of his profession—"never bicker with a balky mule, a tailed-up bull, nor a wild-eyed Injun with a loaded gun." They pulled out as instructed, leaving even their precious tobacco pouches, than which only their matted, long-haired scalps were more dear.

An hour later, full fed for the first time since leaving Fort Reno and driving ahead of them the fresh meat and ammunition-laden packmules of the buffalo hunters, the Cheyenne crossed over the Arkansas. It was the morning of the eighth day of the flight, the 17th of the month.

As the last potbellied Indian pony waded out upon the far bank, Captain J. T. Jackson was a liar by three miles.

Nebraska's Niobrara River lay exactly 497 miles to the north.

CHAPTER 7

FOR FOUR DAYS the Cheyenne position on Major Weston's map went unmarked beyond the Arkansas. While the white-haired C.O. fretted and fumed and held innumerable staff meetings, upwards of four-thousand troops from three army departments converged on west central Kansas to box the fugitives below the Nebraska line.

The military telegraph keys stayed open around the clock. Orders and counterorders flashed from post to post throughout the commands of the Platte, the Canadian and the Arkansas. Field columns from Forts Laramie, Wallace, Lincoln,

Dodge, Leavenworth, Kearney, McPherson, Hays and Riley curried the Kansas plains with a cavalry comb four hundred miles wide and two hundred deep. The Pony Soldiers rode their staggering horses down to the last set of shoes in the ferriers' wagon boxes. Green troopers swore, salty sergeants wept, bedeviled field-grade officers contemplated turning in their oak leaves. All in baffled vain. The Cheyenne had disappeared.

It was the evening of the fifth day before Corporal Feeney once caught up with Weston in the officers' mess and the Major was able to make a new entry in his Indian atlas.

He marked that entry on the Smoky Hill River a hundred miles below the Nebraska border, and marked it with a heavy black X. In that place, six hours earlier, Colonel William H. Lewis had made the strategic blunder of getting between Little Wolf and water that had to be crossed. Colonel Lewis had behind him three companies of mule-mounted infantry, a troop of veteran cavalry, a full supply train of field ambulances and ammunition wagons. He saw in front of him a miserable ragtag of two hundred and fifty Cheyenne women, children and oldsters, headed by no more than fifty starving reservation bucks in cast-off army coats and dirty issue blankets, and all of them caught out in the flat open of a streambed bottomland.

It was a military opportunity complete with the elements of enemy surprise, favorable troop terrain and the clear chance of a field brevet for the lucky commander. He ordered the charge at once and straightaway from the front.

Five minutes later Colonel Lewis had his brevet. But the Cheyenne ball that made him a brigadier was the same one that made his widow eligible for her pension. It came from Wild Hog's borrowed buffalo hunter's rifle, entered beneath his left lung, ranged upward through his spleen and liver, came out beneath his right shoulder blade. He was laid out beneath a packhorse tarpaulin and on his way back to Fort Wallace within the hour.

In a second and third wagon, cursed along in the dust of the first by their anxious drivers, jolted a dozen of his brave boys in blue, each carrying some ounces of Indian lead in addition to his regular equipment, each grinding his teeth on the handiest piece of sling leather to keep from screaming aloud when his hard-axled transport hit an open doghole or caromed off a trailside boulder.

The Cheyenne for their part had taken their first and only

casualty of the march—Tired Horse, an aging subchief who had ridden into the melee with bad medicine and only a broken camp ax, seized from the nearest squaw, with which to strike his futile blow for freedom and the Powder River homelands.

Little Wolf paused neither to mourn his dead nor to make a scalp dance over the enemy's. He pushed his weakening followers across the Smoky Hill that same night. Daylight and four hundred fresh troops from Fort Larned, to the south, found nothing but disappearing travois tracks, half-dried horse droppings and the scattered remains of three campdogs killed for meat and eaten on the march.

The Cheyenne had once more evaporated into the thin prairie air. Again, it was seventy-six hours before Major Howell Weston made another correcting location on his rapidly shrinking map. This time, however, he made it with a different marginal notation. One which seemed to make his previous comments on the Indian approach academic, and to furnish food for frontier thought which even Captain J. T. Jackson found professionally arresting.

From their October 2nd reappearance above Frenchman's Fork of the Republican River in southern Nebraska and through the following days of their crossings of the Kansas Pacific's tracks below Ogallala, the South and North Platte Rivers west of that town, and the Union Pacific's roadbed beyond Sidney Barracks, *the Cheyenne had begun to kill.*

Little Wolf's young men, pressed too hard by the closing troops, desperate alike for fresh horses for themselves and food for their squaws and children, were running murderously out of hand. The narrowing line of their northward flight was now marked, day and night, for the pursuing soldiers. By day, the troops had only to follow the spiraling swing of the buzzards or the slow crawl of the greasy smoke against the afternoon sun. By night it was even easier. Nebraska skies are blacker than the devil's heart when there is no moon. Even a white man can see the midnight blaze of a sod-roof shanty.

Forty miles away and without field glasses.

The woman put the last of the threadbare shirts on the sagging line, turned for the back stoop and another armload of the week's wash. She was a tall woman and might once have been pretty. She walked now with the drudgery of endless hard days pulling at her thin shoulders. Life on the fron-

35

tier fringe of southwestern Nebraska did that to a ten-cow rancher's wife. Life, and the unattended bearing of four children in seven years.

As she moved, head down and listless, a rider came into distant view across the prairie. She looked up, her shoulders straightening. A little smile stirred her lips, spread to her tired eyes. The Third Cavalry's regular dispatch rider, making his weekly trip between Ogallala and Fort Robinson might have seemed small cause for even such minor excitement. Yet for desolate months on end he provided Dutch and Amy Lohburg with their only settlement contact. His coffee stops at their isolated homestead were an important social highlight.

Accordingly, the prairie woman took hurried care to smooth her soiled dress and to push back the moist tangle of her hair. In her pleasure at the rider's approach she did not notice that the dust building behind his laboring mount spelled a full gallop rather than the customary, trailgate lope. But by the time the trooper slid his horse to a stop in front of the sod hut, she had had a long minute in which to study his speed and to find low words for the instinctive fear it called up within her.

"What's the matter, soldier? You look like you'd seen a ghost, or been chased by one." The rider was not the regular courier she had expected but a rawboned giant of a first sergeant she had never seen before. He did not answer her greeting, and her smile made a strained effort to cover her growing apprehension. "Well, get down and come in, mister. Don't just set there. The coffee's on."

Lundy slid off his heaving mount. She had turned for the shanty when his voice caught up with her.

"Miz Lohburg, ma'am, wait up a minute."

"Yes, Sergeant?"

"There ain't no time for coffee. You got to get out of here. Where's the kids?" They had told him about the Lohburgs in Ogallala, ordered him to make sure he warned them on his way up. He saw the quick shadow of his words darken the ranch woman's eyes. She stepped back toward him, hands clenched. "They've come," was all she said. "I knew they would."

Last week's rider had brought the report of the Cheyenne's crossing into Nebraska. Had brought, too, the advice of the command at Sidney Barracks for the out-country settlers to come at once into either Ogallala or Robinson, whichever lay nearest them. But like too many tough frontiersmen before him, Dutch Lohburg had refused to stampede. The hell with the Cheyenne. They were nothing but another thieving pack of redskins that could be handled by any white veteran of the short grass who owned a proper share of guts and a modern repeating rifle. Dutch Lohburg owned both.

"Yes ma'am." Lundy broke the three-second silence. "They sure have. I asked you, Miz Lohburg, where's the kids?" His repeated insistence about the children made sudden, dark sense to Amy Lohburg. Her gray eyes narrowed. "Why don't you ask me where Dutch is?" she said quietly.

"I know where Dutch is, ma'am."

"Oh, no. Oh, dear God, no!"

"He never had a chance, Miz Lohburg. They cut him to pieces. They was after the cattle. I found three fresh hides back in the brush past where I turned Dutch over."

"They were the spring heifers," she murmured. "He'd got the bull and the cows in last week but the heifers hid out on him. He and Billy started out yesterday to—" She broke off hoarsely. "He was with him! Do you hear me, soldier? *Billy was with Dutch!*"

"Not when I found him, he wasn't, ma'am!" Lundy took her roughly by the shoulders. "Now lookit here, Miz Lohburg, don't let down on me. There's a good chance the boy's all right. Then Horse Injuns love boy kids. They likely carted him along with them, not hurt nor nothing."

Amy Lohburg nodded dully. Her eyes were dry as she looked up. "I'll get the girls. They're playing dolls out yonder in the hayshed. We'll take the team and go in the spring-bed wagon."

"I'll hook up the team, ma'am," Lundy threw an anxious glance southward, "then I got to go."

"Thanks, Sergeant, I know you do. Horses are in the back corral with the beefstock." She hesitated, forcing herself to think. "How much time do I have? Where did you find Dutch?"

"Down on that stretch of hay meadow south of the big red butte."

"That's a good half day's ride."

"Yes ma'am. If the Injuns went into camp over the meat from them heifers, you got maybe ten hours yet before they hit here."

"You think they will? Hit here, I mean?"

"Can't miss it. They're after cattle, same as Dutch was. They'll backtrack him to here, looking for more beef."

Amy Lohburg looked at him searchingly. When she spoke there was a grating harshness in her voice. "All right, soldier, God bless you till you're better paid."

She turned away, went swiftly toward the waiting hayshed and the happily aimless chatter of three little girls playing at homemade, rag-stuffed dolls—eighty miles northwest of Ogallala, Nebraska—and less than twenty minutes from Hokomxaaxceta, the slit-eyed War Chief of the Powder River Cheyenne.

Behind the beefstock corral, out past the winter hayshed on Dutch Lohburg's place, a deep drywash ran southward into the lower drainage of Red Butte Meadows. Up out of its cover, ten minutes after the dust of Lundy's horse had died away northward along the Fort Robinson trail, came Little Wolf and three Cheyenne shadows.

They sat their ponies noiseless as the noon-still wind, watching the white woman put the three small children into the rickety wagon. They waited while she carefully covered them with blankets and old feed sacks. They listened approvingly as she admonished them to lie still in their hiding place and not to move no matter what they heard, or what might happen to her.

"He-hau," grunted Left Hand, "the woman is a good mother."

"Aye," agreed Lone Crow. "See how skillfully she hides the little ones. She does not hurry either. She is not afraid."

"She is the wife of the one with the young cattle," grunted Little Wolf. "He was not afraid either."

The fourth Cheyenne said nothing. Twelve-year-old boys did not offer scout-party opinions among the Cut Arm People. Not when they rode with the War Chief. Red Bird held his counsel.

"Well," shrugged Lone Crow, "how will it go with these? We had better not let them get away. The woman looks strong, like a good traveler. She would probably get to Fort Robinson all right."

"Hau," growled Left Hand. "Then we will have all those cursed Pony Soldiers from up there knowing where to look for us. We had better kill her, I guess."

"We do not have to hurt the children though," amended Lone Crow. "There's no use in that. We can give them to Red

38

Bird's mother. She has the little boy anyway." He turned to the silent Little Wolf. "How do you see it, Hokom-xaaxceta?"

Little Wolf did not answer at once but young Red Bird shivered at the cold look he was wearing. It took more courage than anything he had ever done, yet he pushed his pony forward unhesitatingly. "May I have a word, uncle?" he asked. The brooding Cheyenne leader looked at him, answered slowly. "You have ridden well. You have not complained. Say it."

"*Haho*, thank you," murmured the boy. He touched the fingertips of his left hand to his brow in the Cheyenne gesture of deep respect. Then, clearly and quietly, "I say it is not the way of chiefs to be afraid of women."

"And I say it is not the place of sniveling boys to advise warriors!" snapped Left Hand. Lone Crow started to open his slack mouth to agree but Little Wolf cut him off. "Don't say any more," he advised them. "I have made up my mind. Our nephew has a young head with an old tongue in it. Boy," he went on, "you go tell that woman that we will not harm her but that we need her wagon to carry all this meat in." He gestured over his shoulder toward the corral. "There are seven fat cattle in that pen."

"Thank you, uncle!" Red Bird's smile lit up his round face. "What more may I tell her?"

"That we will trade her Left Hand's and Lone Crow's ponies for her fine team of big horses. That she is to put the children on one pony and take the other for herself. That she is to go at once and not look back and that she must be a long ways from here when my young men come up."

"Yes, uncle. Is there no more?"

"What more would you have, boy?"

"She is but a woman. What if she does not know the way to the fort?"

Little Wolf looked at him, quick and sharp. The trace of what might have been a smile moved his cruel mouth. "You are reminding me that you *do* know the way, is that it, Soft Heart?"

"Never, uncle!" Red Bird drew himself up. "I am a warrior. You have said it yourself."

"Well, 'warrior,'" ordered Little Wolf, "if the woman does not know the way, you will take the lead rope of her children's pony and show it to her."

"I go!" replied the boy proudly. Then, to Left Hand and Lone Crow with an imperious wave of his small arm, "You heard the War Chief. Give me your horses." The two amazed braves had only time to gather the angry wind into their mouths, no time at all to spit it back out. "That is right," observed Little Wolf, tapping the breech of his Winchester significantly, *"you heard the War Chief."*

His two murderous followers had been long in the service of Hokom-xaaxceta. Long enough, by all Indian odds, to recognize the too-quiet way he always began to talk when the parley had reached the point where his lean fingers started that ominous drumbeat on his rifle breech.

"Aye, we heard, brother"—they slid off their ponies with the sullen admission—"but you are getting as soft in the head as the boy is in the heart."

Little Wolf watched Red Bird lead the two mounts quickly around the ranchhouse. He waited until he reappeared in front of it and the startled woman looked up in reply to his greeting. He still waited while Amy Lohburg swung her frightened gaze across the ridgepole of the shanty and fastened it upon his own gaunt figure. Only when he had raised his left hand, the palm out toward her in the Plains Indian sign of peaceful intent, and she had seen it and turned in quick relief to Red Bird, did he bother to speak further to his scowling companions.

"The day," he said to them, "that sees Hokom-xaaxceta soft in the head will look down upon such bravehearts as you, many long moons at rest beneath the buffalo grass."

CHAPTER 8

LIEUTENANT FRANK FERRIS, Weston's acting A.G., looked up from his desk in the C.O.'s outer office as Lundy entered. He returned the latter's salute, took the dispatch pouch, broke its seal, leafed through its contents. "Nothing—as usual," he said disinterestedly. "Anything new on the Indians on your way up?"

"Nope. They were right behind me out of Ogallala, that's all I know."

"You mean you actually spotted them?"

"No, just saw where they'd killed some cattle. Anything new here?"

"Nothing past Ogallala. They seem to have faded out for good this time. We won't see anything of them up here. Jackson's right about that. They'll turn west and run for the Powder. Good night, Sergeant."

"Yes sir." Lundy made no move to go.

Ferris glanced up. "I said good night, soldier."

"Yes sir," Lundy saluted, "I'd like to see the C.O., Lieutenant."

"No luck." The adjutant waved the dismissal irritably, inclining his head toward the closed door behind him. "The Major's not to be disturbed. Bringing his little map up to date, you know."

"Yes sir, I know. I'd like to see him anyway."

Ferris straightened. "Listen, Lundy, when I say good night and the Major's busy, you get the hell out, you hear me?" Further insubordination was averted by Howell Weston's silvery head poking apologetically through the opening crack of his door. "Someone to see me, Frank?" he inquired hopefully.

"Me, sir." Lundy saluted smartly, taking no chances. "I won't be a minute, Major."

"Well, come in, man, come in. We've always got a minute for a good soldier, haven't we, Lieutenant?"

"Apparently we have," complained Ferris, and watched the door close behind the two with a low four-letter growl never meant for majors' ears.

There seemed to be no end to this Weston's coddling of the men. Ever since his arrival at Robinson it had become a bad joke among the junior brass that corporals were outranking captains. Ordinarily, such army humor would have served to gloss over a fussy old staff officer's ignorance of the hard facts of frontier combat discipline. But not when that old staffer's second-in-command was named J. T. Jackson. The Captain was a spring-steel Academy ramrod. The looseness in enlisted respect inspired by Weston's fatherly attitude toward the ranks infuriated him, and when Jackson was mad he rode Frank Ferris and all the rest of the staff with a straight bar bit and six-inch reins.

For the moment, young Ferris shook off his upset without too great an effort. Digging his last letter from the girl back home out of his blouse pocket, he began rereading it for the fifteenth time since mail call.

Had he troubled to put his ear to the Major's door he might have had a little less success with his control.

"Well, sir, that's the way it was," Lundy was concluding soberly. "I found Dutch shot up like I said, hooked up the team for Miz Lohburg and come on in with my dispatches. That was noon yesterday."

"I see," said Weston slowly. He thought a moment, then added, "It looks like we had the right idea putting you on in the regular rider's place, doesn't it? If that poor woman and her children get away they can thank your Cherokee ancestors, I'd say."

"Yes sir, maybe they might. But that ain't helping them none right now, Major."

Weston looked at him. "I know, I know," he frowned. "Now let me get this straight, Lundy. You think there's a good chance this Mrs. Lohburg may have gotten clear of the ranch, might now be somewhere along the trail between here and there? And that if we start soon enough there's some possibility we can find her in time. Is that about it?"

"I hope to God it is, Major. Miz Lohburg she's as fine a little woman as I've ever seen and them little girls of hers are that sweet and pretty, every one of them, that it'd break your heart. I only thought that if I could talk to you personal, you might see fit to go out after them. I reckon maybe I shouldn't have bothered though. It don't sound too smart, standing here, to talk of chasing off into them Sand Hills with the hostiles closing in like they are."

Weston shook his head. "I'm afraid that's right, Lundy."

"Yes sir, I thought it would be." He saluted stiffly. "Thanks for seeing me, Major."

"On the other hand," continued Weston, staring into his favorite empty corner of the room and tapping his desktop absent mindedly, "if I were smart half the time and right the other half, I'd be a brigadier by now."

"Sir?" Lundy swung around, not daring to believe what he thought had just been said.

"I think you heard me, John. Send Meeker over here and never mind passing the time of night with Lieutenant Ferris on your way out." Lundy looked at him, his broad face suffused with gratitude. He stepped awkwardly toward the desk.

"Lord love you, Major," he said simply. "I reckon that means we'll start out first thing in the morning."

"I reckon it means better than that, John," Weston smiled. "If you'll stop standing there soliciting the Lord in my behalf, we'll start in twenty minutes."

He followed the big noncom into the outer office, waited for him to get out of the room, spoke unhurriedly to Lieutenant Ferris. "Meeker will be over here in a minute, Frank. When he shows up, send him on to my quarters. Close up here and go to bed, boy. On your way stop by Jackson's quarters and leave this order—"

"Yes sir," said Ferris, glad enough to be off night duty by 10 P.M., where Weston generally kept his A.G.'s up till daylight. "What order, Major?"

"Tell him to take command until I get back. Under no circumstance is he to take any troops off the post. Is that clear?"

"Of course, sir." Ferris's curiosity was beginning to sit up and take a little nourishment. "May I ask where you're going?"

"You may," grinned Weston happily. "However, it won't do you any good."

"Yes sir," replied the younger officer, not amused. "Anything else to tell the Captain?"

"As a matter of fact, yes."

Weston looked straight at his disgruntled adjutant, took his map out of his pocket, refolded it deliberately, put it back with studied care, said it in such a flint-edged way no man could misunderstand exactly what he meant.

"You may tell Captain Jackson that I have taken Sergeants Lundy and Meeker and a picked squad of pencil sharpeners ninety miles down the Ogallala trail to bring my Indian artwork up to date."

Red Bird had been to the agency schools at both Red Cloud and Darlington. Dull Knife had made him go. In the old chief's mind it was only wise that the youth who would one day replace him as tribal leader of the Northern Cheyenne should grow skillful in the tongue of his people's conquerors. In his quick, bright way Red Bird had done his grandfather's bidding. He had learned good English and learned it very fast, as only the young may do with an alien speech.

As he spoke to Amy Lohburg now, in the late afternoon of the second day of their flight he was glad he had, for it was suddenly important that the brave white woman understand what he said. "Lady," he had called her that from the beginning, "you take this child now." He had carried the smallest girl, a lisping baby of three, on his own pony all the way from the ranch. He passed her quickly over to her mother as he spoke, then handed Amy the lead rope of the second mount, as well. "You hold this pony, too," he directed calmly. "I am going back a little ways and look at something."

He wheeled his pony, then checked him, with the added warning, "Do not move out of these small trees here. And have the children to be very quiet while I am gone."

"What is it, Red Bird?" she asked. "Are we being followed?"

"I think so, lady. But do not move."

With that he was gone. Amy Lohburg was left alone with her three small children and the late afternoon stillness of a creekside cottonwood grove. They were eight miles south of the Niobrara River, forty-eight southwest of Fort Robinson.

Red Bird was back in half an hour. It seemed to Amy as though he had been gone a year. But her relief at again seeing the cheerful little Indian boy lived less than thirty seconds. "Come a little this way, please," he told her. "The children should not hear this. Put the little one on the pony with the others."

They moved their mounts away. Red Bird spoke rapidly, making unconscious use of his hands in the fluent Cheyenne way. "They are seven," he said. "Left Hand and Lone Crow, who I could tell by the color of their horses though they were yet far away, and five young men. These I could tell by the hard way they handled their ponies. They are after *us*, lady."

The terror of it leaped into Amy's eyes but she kept her voice down. "How can they be? You said Little Wolf wouldn't follow us. You told me he gave you his word."

"Little Wolf *is not* following us, lady."

"Why these others, then?" She wanted to believe the boy but her fear made her challenge him. "You said Little Wolf was their war chief. If he told them to let us alone, surely they wouldn't disobey him."

"Indians are different," said the boy. "They are not like the Pony Soldiers. Every Cheyenne is his own chief when he wants to be. That is just the way it is. My uncle told them to let us alone. I heard him. But he has many troubles now. Many squaws and old people to watch over. He cannot hold all his young men every minute."

44

"But Red Bird—"

"You must listen to me, lady. I know my people. Left Hand and Lone Crow are not young men but they are angry with me. They have gotten those others to come along with them. Even so they are not bad Indians, they are only afraid. They do not understand the white people like my uncle, Little Wolf, understands them. They fear to let you talk to the Pony Soldiers at Fort Robinson. Do you see how it is?"

"No, no!" said Amy distractedly. "I still can't see—"

The Cheyenne youth straightened, scowling at her in sudden Indian anger. "Now you talk too much. Like a woman. You do as I say or your little boy will not see you again."

He had told her that seven-year-old Billy Lohburg was safe in the care of his own mother, and that Dull Knife had said the boy would be delivered at Fort Robinson unharmed. The knowledge of this let her know precisely what the Indian boy meant when he said Billy would not see her again if she persisted in the delay.

"I'm sorry, Red Bird," she murmured. "What is it you want us to do?"

"You will see. Follow me fast now, leading the pony with all the children on it."

They went out of the grove on a bouncing trot, heading for the trail's crossing of the small Niobrara tributary. In midstream the Cheyenne youth turned his pony up the center of the rocky creekbed. Desperately, Amy followed him, using both hands to hang on to the lead rope of the third pony, her own mount chopping along surefooted and without guidance in the path of Red Bird's.

Twilight shut swiftly in. Still the Indian boy kept the ponies stumbling up the streambed. It was not until he found a long slope of sandstone bordering the creek that he took the horses out of the water.

Beyond the sandstone was a low prairie swale, thickly grassed and overgrown with scrub willows. Into this he guided Amy and the children. "Take the blankets off your pony," he ordered low voiced. "Put the children to rest on the ground there. Tell them it is time to sleep. Cover them up. Sing to them. Do it very softly. They must sleep quick but there can be no noise. Do you understand me, lady?"

"You mean they might still follow us?"

"There is no doubt, lady. Our tracks do not cross the water back there."

Amy swallowed hard. She started to say something, thought better of it, swallowed again, went swiftly to work. When she had the children safely bedded and their fretful complaints of cold and hunger quieted, Red Bird moved quickly. Snubbing each of the ponies to a willow sapling, he bound their muzzles with their horsehair surcingles, repeated his low warning to Amy, crept back through the willow scrub to the edge of the swale overlooking the creekbed. Here he waited, peering intently down the darkening stream and thinking hard Indian thoughts.

It was now only a matter of the race between full darkness and the drying of the water tracks of their ponies where they came out of the creek across the sandstone outcropping. That and seven other small things.

The race was very close.

Those seven other small things made it that way.

They came splashing and cursing up the course of the stream only minutes later. Red Bird carefully counted the headfeathered shadows. He came out with the right number. And when they halted in midstream to wrangle their future course a bit, any knowing eye could see from the way those feathers slanted down at the backs of the silhouetted heads that those seven shadowy things out there were very solid Powder River Cheyenne.

Warrior or no warrior, Red Bird's stomach curled up and crawled in under his shrinking brisket.

"Now listen," growled Left Hand, "talk will not catch them. We will go on up the water a ways, then some of us will come back down each side and we will jump them out wherever they are. But we have to go far enough up this stream to make sure we get above them. *Nohetto*, that is all there is to it. Let's go."

"I still think we ought to look in those willow trees over there." Lone Crow said it with his hand pointing right at the hidden Red Bird. "No!" barked one of the young warriors. "I'm going with Left Hand. He is right. We can't waste good time looking under every bush between here and the Niobrara. We can search into those willow trees on the way back." There was another bad moment of grumbling, then all six shadows swung their ponies to follow Left Hand upstream—and Red Bird let out a breath he had been holding until his head grew dizzy.

When he got back to the white woman he found her crouched over the children, alert and watchful. He knelt beside her in the darkness. Gently lifting the blanket, he looked beneath it. All three little girls were asleep. He shifted his glance to Amy. "Wake them up," he whispered, "and be very still about it."

"But the Indians have gone on," she objected. "I heard them splashing up the creek. Oh, Red Bird, can't we let them rest just a little while?"

"Wake them up, lady," repeated the Cheyenne boy. "A little while is all we have."

"You mean they will be coming back?" said Amy, wide-eyed.

"Very soon now. They spoke of these trees and said they would look into them without fail."

"But what can we do now? Where can we go?"

Red Bird caught the unsteadiness beginning to get into the white woman's voice. He forced a confidence he did not feel into his own words. "We can run now, lady. Straight for Fort Robinson. And very fast."

"No, we can't, we can't!" despaired Amy. "My children can't ride fast, Red Bird."

"They will learn," said Red Bird with Indian bluntness. As he said it he unsheathed his knife, cut his mount's picket rope into three equal pieces. "With its feet tied under a good pony's belly," he nodded quietly, "even a white child will find it hard to fall off."

CHAPTER 9

IT WAS a quiet night, clear as handblown glass, cold as a dead man's breath. The motionless glitter of the Nebraska stars gave only enough light for the shivering troopers to see the back-flung wave of Major Weston's yellow gauntlet. They pulled their horses in, crowding them close for warmth, waiting while the three figures ahead of them talked in low voices.

"How far along are we now, Lundy?"

"About thirty miles. We're just into the Sand Hills. That

makes it right at ten miles to the river, somewheres around and even forty from the fort."

"I see. Strike a light here, will you, Meeker?"

Meeker scratched a match, cupped it while Weston studied his watch. "Eleven-ten," he announced thoughtfully. "Well, boys, where do we go from here?"

"I dunno, Major," offered Lundy. "If they haven't lost the trail or been caught up to from behind, we should have rode into them before now."

"Meeker?"

"I'll play those, sir. Lundy, here, says the Lohburg woman had a light wagon and a good team. She's had since noon yesterday to use them. Chances are we're too late." He paused, added uneasily, "Save for maybe giving them a Christian burial."

Weston put his watch away. "Lundy," he said quietly, "how do you play your hunches?"

"All the way," grunted the big sergeant. "What you getting at, Major?"

"I've got a hunch this woman is still alive."

"So?"

"So we'll play it like you say, Lundy—all the way. Meeker—"

"Yes sir."

"We passed a straggle of cottonwoods back a bit. Break the men out and gather up all the dry wood you can find. Tote it up here on the double. I'm going to build a bonfire."

"Good God, Major!" Meeker's shocked grunt came out of him like somebody had struck him across the kidneys with a riflebutt, "not with these lousy hills full of homesick hostiles!"

"From what Lundy says," rapped Weston, "that woman and those poor kids are either lost and still alive, or they're dead. If they're lost the fire may bring them in to us. If they're dead it may bring somebody else in to us. It's what we call a calculated risk at staff headquarters, Sergeant. Get going."

"Yes sir," muttered Meeker. And got going.

Within five minutes the first armload of dry twigs was being fanned alive by two very disconcerted first sergeants. Within ten, some bigger limbs had been piled on and Lundy was backing away from the blaze, batting at its rising shower of sparks with his field hat and cursing the day that found poor old Colonel McAllister's insides giving out on him and little Hollie Wes-

48

ton standing ready and waiting to take over the command at the nearby city of Lincoln.

"Don't slow your pony now, lady. Don't hold him back. Just let him go." With the quick reassurance, Red Bird waved ahead through the starlight to the dark gleam of the main Niobrara. "It is wide, all right, but very shallow. Good bottom all the way."

Amy Lohburg said nothing, only tightened her hand on the halter rope of her Cheyenne mount. The hour when she might question the Indian boy's judgment had passed in the sixty chilling seconds she had hovered over her sleeping children back in that cottonwood grove, while Left Hand and Lone Crow argued the point of searching the trees right then, or on their way back downstream.

Seeing her lean obediently forward along her pony's neck, Red Bird grinned. Reaching out in the darkness he slashed the loping animal across the rump with his rawhide quirt. At the same moment it leaped into its startled gallop, he dug his heels into his own pony's ribs, rasped a sibilant Cheyenne *"Hee-yahhh!"* back at the children's pony, raced all three mounts in a driving, rock-showering run straight at the Fort Robinson crossing of the Niobrara.

They were across the forbidding stretch of black water and safely out the far side in ten snorting jumps. But it was only when the ponies had let back down into their customary lope and the frightened youngsters had stopped whimpering, that Amy could ease the aching clamp of her jaw muscles enough to speak to Red Bird.

"How far have we come since they passed us back there on that creek?" she asked hopelessly.

"Nearly ten miles, lady. We are doing well."

It was just a little lie. He felt Maheo would understand and forgive it.

"Then how much farther is it to the fort? I can't stand much more, Red Bird. I'm all sick and shaky inside. I just can't hold on much longer."

The Cheyenne boy's answer came with deliberate harshness. "You are a grown woman, lady. Do you want your feet tied like a child's?"

The bite of the question angered her, as he had meant it to. She straightened a little, clung still more desperately to her pony's dripping sides. Teeth set, she fought down the torture in her trembling thighs, where the saddleless friction of the animal's ribs had scraped the skin away to the raw flesh. "Do you think they are very close after us?" She asked it better now, her voice not so high. Red Bird nodded, satisfied.

"No, not yet. When they are we will know it. Don't worry about them," he repeated the lie, "we are doing well."

They rode for perhaps fifteen minutes, getting another two miles up the trail before it happened.

One moment they were going along with the prairie all silent and peaceful around them, and with the faintest pulse of hope beginning to steady the pounding of Amy Lohburg's heart. The next moment, a single eerie wolf howl was stabbing out of the night from the backtrail direction of the Niobrara. In the third moment Red Bird was slipping free the wrist-thong of his quirt, getting its heavy butt firmly in his small hand, slicing its leathers once more across the rump of Amy's pony.

"Now we *really* run, lady!" he shouted.

"Hee-yahhh, hee-yahhh!" he yelped at the children's pony, jerking its lead rope and flailing his own mount with the quirt, using it butt-first and mercilessly now. The time for holding in the horses and keeping the voices down, that time was far past. Now it was a horse race for sure—and not likely to be a very long one.

He forced his pony up alongside Amy's, shouldering him in close so that she might see his smile and take strength from it. "That is them back there," he called cheerfully. "We Cheyennes always howl like that when the trail grows warm, like a wolf. Like that back there. You hear it, lady?" Amy heard it all right. All seven of those Cheyenne wolves were yelping and crying along the trail, making the night full of their hideous noise, and making it sound as though they were thirty yards to the south, not three miles or more. "Oh, Red Bird, Red Bird!" she gasped. "We'll never make it now!"

He shook his head, forcing the bright smile. The third lie was the biggest one of all but he told it well. "We will, we will!" he shouted. "See, now, the ponies are running stronger than ever!" They were running stronger than ever, he knew, because they were bred to run that way. Until they dropped dead. He knew, as well, just about how many miles they were from doing just that.

It was three. Maybe four. Not over five.

Fort Robinson was forty.

Three things were running on white man's time that night, not on Cheyenne's.

Red Bird's courage.

Amy Lohburg's out-settlement toughness.

Major Howell Weston's stemwinding pocket watch.

Fifteen minutes after the Indian boy's desperate last quirting of the failing Cheyenne ponies, and with his final request having just been made of Maheo to let him die in a way his fierce uncle would approve, the Cut Arm People's god sent Little Wolf's nephew a very big medicine sign. Not a mile up the Fort Robinson trail, the sky grew suddenly bright. It started tiny and dull red, no bigger than a small brave's hand, then built swiftly into a leaping flare of orange-yellow. It meant, in the time and place and from the careless way it had been lit, only one thing to the mind of the Plains Indian youth.

"Pony Soldiers!" yelled Red Bird, letting it come out like a mixed war cry and boyish whoop of triumph rolled into one. *"He-hau Maheo!"*

In Cheyenne, the last part of it meant a heartfelt "thank God," but Amy Lohburg did not need to understand Cheyenne or the last part of it. She was a short-grass rancher's widow. What she understood was the English, first part of it. With seven Horse Indians riding up on you forty miles from the nearest fort, "Pony Soldiers!" was a shout that needed no translation.

She beat at her staggering pony with her bare hands, laughed hysterically and shouted aloud to her own God and in her own wild language. She was still laughing and crying when her pony stumbled for the last time and went down with its nose in the ashes of Major Weston's signal fire. Behind her mount, the tough little pinto mare which had carried her three children seventy miles in less than thirty-six hours jogged to a stop and stood blowing, head down, nostrils belled and bleeding.

The mare had enough strength remaining to follow Sergeant Lundy's frantic hauling on her lead rope, on into the troopers' camp, and to stand quietly while Weston and Meeker cut her belly ropes and pulled the three sobbing children free of her trembling back. Then, still quietly, she put her muzzle to the ground and went down, knees first, beside the first pony. She was dead in twenty fluttering breaths.

For a bad half hour Lundy and his cursing squad bellied into the fireside dirt, spraying Springfield lead at Left Hand's and Lone Crow's angry young men while Weston restrained the hysterical Amy Lohburg and Meeker cuddled her frightened children behind the shelter of the dead ponies. Past that time the Cheyenne, knowing when they had been outguessed by their War Chief's favorite nephew and furthermore knowing when they were outgunned by the thrice-damned Pony Soldiers, broke off the firelit shooting match and faded into the south-trail shadows.

But even when Amy had quieted down enough to tell her story to Major Weston and his silent men, and no matter the following hours of hopeful waiting and watching into the outer darkness, the eighth Cheyenne did not reappear.

They stared the night away at the empty blackness of the prairie. It only stared them back.

Nohetto, there was nothing out there.

Red Bird was gone.

CHAPTER 10

TONO'ISHI, the month of the Cool Moon, was gone. It was nineteen days into *Hissikevinhis,* the Dust and Dirt-Blowing Moon, when Little Wolf halted the Cheyenne column for the last time and waved Dull Knife and the elder chiefs forward. The place was the south bank of the same small Niobrara tributary up which Red Bird had led Amy Lohburg and her children in escaping Left Hand and Lone Crow. The time was another sunset as gray and cold as that one. And as lonely as the whistle of the October wind.

When Dull Knife came up to him, Little Wolf motioned the other chiefs to draw their ponies back a little and to one side so that he and the old man could talk alone.

"Well, father," he said softly, "what do you think of this place?"

"This is a good place," said the old chief. "The people are tired, the ponies are tired, I am tired. We will camp here."

"All right," nodded Little Wolf, "it will be as you say. But after we have camped we will talk. Is that agreed, father?"

"It is agreed. I will tell the women to unpack the poles."

An hour later the last lodge was in place, the last cook-fire kindled, the last shreds of rotting bone and bloody hide from the Lohburg cattle simmering in the boiling pots. When the final ladle of the putrid broth had been apportioned to the women and children, the chiefs and elder warriors tightened their loincloths, lit their pipes, sat back to await the results of the council now going forward in Dull Knife's tipi.

The long minutes crawled away. Still, the closed entrance flaps of the old chief's lodge did not open. The waiting grew unbearable as the fires died and the haranguing of the squaws and fitful, hungry crying of their cradle-board infants withdrew beneath the muffling cover of the lodgeskins. In the ensuing stillness the contending voices within Dull Knife's lodge rose and fell in guttural Cheyenne argument, the one, deep and forceful and increasingly heated, the other, slow, patient and continuingly restrained.

Presently they ceased altogether.

The entrance flaps moved and parted.

Little Wolf, head high, jaw set, strode toward the fire and the circle of uneasy subchiefs surrounding it. Behind him came Dull Knife, walking like an old man, his chin upon his bear-claw necklace, the wrinkles of his leathered face showing the full count of his fifty-eight years.

At the fire's edge the War Chief halted, waiting for Dull Knife to come up and be seated first. Only when the latter had found his place in the circle and scraped up a coal for his pipe did he take his own place directly across from him. He said nothing, still waiting while the elder chief drew his smoke into life and puffed four mouthfuls of it to the sacred quarters of the compass. Then he touched his brow to the aging tribal leader and began to speak. For all the harsh set of his dark face, his words fell with a peculiar sadness.

"We have come to a parting of the trail, my father and I," he announced. "He has his eyes in one direction, I see only the other. Let him tell it. I give you my place at the fire, father."

Dull Knife sat, unmoving. He smoked for a full minute and until the spittle sucked into the stem of his pipe and its lighting coal faltered and went out. "I am an old man," he said at last. "I honor each of you and above all I touch the brow to Hokom-xaaxceta. Still, he speaks the truth. From this smoke we ride no more together, he and I." He pointed toward the War Chief with the stem of his pipe. "I give you back your place at the fire. Tell them how it is with us and how it must be for them."

Little Wolf gave no more time to ceremony then. He spoke quickly, tolling off for the silent subchiefs the lateness of the hour which lay upon the Powder River Cheyenne. "Dull Knife says that we are home already, that the long march is over. That he will camp here beside this water and await, in peace, the coming of the Pony Soldiers. He says he trusts the white man and thinks we will be allowed to stay here this time. He says he is thinking much of the kindness and good heart of Three Stars Crook, who treated us so well at Fort Robinson before. He thinks Three Stars will speak again to the Grand-father in Washington and that after that all the Cheyenne can stay here and hunt the buffalo and live among the pines and mountains as before."

The stillness which followed was a tangible thing. It shut in over the little fire and the scowling Cheyenne, close and bad-aired as a lathered blanket. It was Tangled Hair who narrowed his slant eyes and said it for them all.

"And what," he growled, "does Hokom-xaaxceta say?"

"I say a white dog does not change color simply because the snow is coming," Little Wolf quoted an old Cheyenne proverb. "I do not trust the Pony Soldiers and I will not wait here for them."

"Is that all you say?" demanded Lone Crow querulously.

"No, I say more. All of you had better hear it, too."

"We are listening," mumbled Left Hand discourteously, "but hurry it along. It is getting cold here."

"Listen well, then!" barked Little Wolf. "We are free now. If we fight them they will honor us. We can make a real peace. One they will remember. If we go into them crying 'See us now. We surrender like women. We are hungry and weak for food,' they will laugh at us and send us back to the hot coun-try." He paused, sweeping the circle with his piercing glance. "Remember what I say, my brothers. Remember it a long time. Peace is never put into the laps of beggars. It is seized only by the hands of warriors."

Again the uneasy silence fell upon the subchiefs. Its embar-rassed heaviness grew until Bull Hump could stand it no longer. "That is all very well, cousin," he muttered. "Fine words, a big speech. But what about Three Stars? We know his heart is good for us. You have not answered that part of it."

"Aye," sighed Little Wolf bitterly, "Three Stars—"

"Well?" insisted Bull Hump.

"You fools!" hissed the War Chief. "His heart was good for us before, too. Your memories are not long enough to tie a good knot in. Three Stars argued with the Grandfather in Washington that other time. We still went south when the orders came back to the Pony Soldiers."

"Oh, surely," said Left Hand quickly. "We remember that all right. But maybe this time the Grandfather will listen and we will not go back."

"Yes," agreed his friend Lone Crow, "I think that, too."

"I say yes, also," muttered Wild Hog, and turned his eyes away from Little Wolf.

"And I," concluded Little Chief importantly. He touched the doeskin carrying case of the Medicine Arrows to bolster his claim. "My medicine tells me it is a true thing. This time the Grandfather will listen to Three Stars. The arrows say that."

The respected opinion of their Arrow Keeper was enough for the remaining three members of the nine-man council. Blacksmith, Noisy Walking and Big Beaver indicated their awkward agreement without finding words for it. Or perhaps not wanting to find those words, what with the way Little Wolf was looking at them.

The War Chief let them all freeze a long time under the frost of that stare. He waited until the last man had turned his eyes away and hung his head in mumbling shame. Then he only nodded to Little Chief. "All right, my brother, it is time for the sticks."

The elders shifted uncomfortably.

In the Cheyenne way of doing such things there was no easy equivalent of the white man's secret ballot. When the trail grew narrow and the blind canyon of a bad decision finally trapped him, a warrior had to stand up and be counted. Among the Cut Arm electorate you did not simply hide your heart in a folded piece of paper and drop it safely into a guarded box.

There was no sound as Little Chief brought out the buckskin quiver which contained the voting sticks. Not a moccasin shuffled as he passed it around the voting circle. Each chief took one of the pointed, foot-long shafts of polished cedar. Only Dull Knife and Little Wolf sat with folded arms and let the quiver pass, untouched.

This was a vote of war or peace. If a man meant to go with

Little Wolf along the former trail, he would thrust his stick upright in the ground before the War Chief. If he meant to stay with Dull Knife on the latter path, he would simply lay it on the ground in front of himself, point toward the fire.

Quickly the vote went around the circle. Nothing further of bitterness or anger revealed itself in Little Wolf's face as the polished bits of wood came down. But when the ninth stick was placed, not one stood upright. All pointed toward the fire and away from war and Little Wolf. There was a silence then which made the former pauses seem like thunderclaps. In the dead center of this new stillness, a slight, boyish form stepped out of the surrounding darkness into the fading glow of the council fire.

"Cowards!" cried the small newcomer furiously, and stalked across the circle without another look for its startled members. Haughtily, he seated himself at the War Chief's side. No man moved, nor said him nay, as he pulled from his hunting quiver a single, gaudily feathered arrow.

"Enitoeme, I honor him!" said Dull Knife's grandson.

And he drove the quivering shaft, full upright, into the ground in front of Little Wolf.

CHAPTER 11

RED BIRD lay awake in the gloom of his mother's tipi. Sleep would not come, but the thoughts which were too many and too unhappy for the mind of a twelve-year-old boy would.

He stared across the darkened lodge, not seeing the dim, blanketed forms of his mother, his two young sisters and the captive white boy, Billy Lohburg. He was still seeing the look which had come over his grandfather's face when he had broken into the council of elders to say the courage-word and to jam his arrow into the dirt in front of Little Wolf. It was, he thought, as though he had plunged his skinning knife into the old chief's heart rather than a harmless hunting arrow into the ground at his uncle's feet.

Dull Knife had said nothing to him, nor had Little Wolf.

They had both only sat still, looking far away across the fire while the other chiefs had gotten up and stalked away to their lodges. Finally, they too had arisen and gone away, leaving Red Bird alone with his small-boy fears of the punishment that was certain to come with daylight.

The worst of it was that Little Wolf had not touched nor taken up the arrow. He had gone away without bearing it with him as custom demanded he should if he approved its giver's offer. Red Bird had dared the love of Dull Knife and the anger of all the other chiefs to say that he would follow his fierce uncle. And Little Wolf had refused his voting stick.

The Cheyenne boy was still awake when the frosty autumn sun rolled up from beyond the Sand Hills. He started nervously when he thought he heard the fall of a moccasin outside the lodge, then felt his belly draw up like green rawhide when the entrance flaps parted and Dull Knife peered into the tipi's darkness.

"I am here, grandfather," he managed bravely. "I have been waiting for you."

"Shhh!" cautioned the old chief, putting a warning finger to his lips. "Come on out to the fire, boy. Quickly now, before the squaws begin stirring about. We must talk, you and I."

Red Bird got up, tiptoed past his mother and the sleeping white boy. He shivered uncontrollably as the entrance flaps fell together behind him, and the chill was not born in the bite of the October dawn. Yet he came to the fire with his head up and his step firm as a chief's grandson should.

Dull Knife had melted some creek ice in a small pot and steeped some shags of willow bark in it. He offered the boy a buffalo horn cup of the acrid beverage. Red Bird took it and drank it gratefully. "He-hau," he said politely, handing the empty horn back to the old man. "I am ready now, grandfather."

"We must hurry," nodded Dull Knife. "Listen well, boy.

"I have two good ponies tethered behind my lodge, the black mare and the roan gelding. I want you to go now and get the white boy and take those ponies and ride out of here. Last night after the sticks were passed many of the young men heard the way it went against Hokum-xaaxceta and did not like it. Your uncle is going west, on into the mountains out there beyond the Powder. A lot of the people are going with him. I do not think it will be good for the white boy to be around here."

"Do you want me to take him to the fort?" asked Red Bird, big-eyed. "The way you promised?"

"Aye, to the fort," replied the old man. "The way I promised."

"All right, grandfather. But there is one thing before I go—" The boy trailed off the words and Dull Knife motioned him to be quick and to speak up. He gulped, put his small hand hesitantly on the old chief's bony knuckles, said it in a little voice and very quietly. "Grandfather, why did you turn away from me last night? Why did you not speak to me?"

Dull Knife folded the slim red hand in his. He shook his head, blinking to get the sting and the water of the morning fire's smoke out of his eyes. "Because my heart was too full," he said softly. "I could not look at you because I was so proud. There was nothing to say. *Nohetto,* boy, you had said it all."

For a moment Red Bird could not reply. His throat hurt and it would not work so that the words came up out of it as they should. Then he straightened his shoulders. "But if this were so, grandfather, why did my uncle leave the arrow in the ground?"

Neither of them had heard the lean shadow which had drifted up to stand behind them. Both flinched and swung around as the familiar, deep voice answered for itself. "I left it there for all to see," growled Little Wolf. "No one will touch it now, either. When these fires are cold and this camp is forgotten that arrow will still be there. Right where it is now. Where a real Cheyenne put it. And where his War Chief left it to honor him."

Red Bird's heart pounded until it seemed it must burst his ribs. The pride of it was more than an Indian boy could bear. He could say nothing. Do nothing. Only stand and stare at his War Chief.

Little Wolf was in full war-trail regalia. He had on his best hunting shirt, beaded and quilled in a blaze of color and strung with dyed horsehair and ermine tails from shoulder to wrist. His long hair was meticulously braided, its single glossy coil hanging across his right shoulder after the Northern Cheyenne fashion. He wore his famed head circlet of black otter fur. The burnished silver cross which was his dreaded battle charm glowed resplendent upon his breast. With his skull-thin face, narrow eyes, broken-bridged nose, cruel, knife-scarred mouth and Negro-dark skin, he towered in the breathless eye of Red Bird's imagination like a great black giant against the

Preserve the legacy of the Old West in distinctive hardcover volumes...

THE LOUIS L'AMOUR COLLECTION

Now you and your family can experience the authentic Old West...its rich lore and legend in a rugged, handsome series: The Louis L'Amour Collection—superb hardcover Heritage Editions, meticulously bound in padded Sierra-brown leatherette.

Each matching volume—with the look and feel of hand-rubbed saddle leather—is an enduring testament to our unique American past...a tribute to the narrative power of Louis L'Amour, the most popular writer of frontier adventures who ever lived.

Start your Louis L'Amour Collection now with FLINT—a gripping novel of murder and revenge—FREE for 10 days. If you decide to keep it, further volumes may be previewed each month, also for 10 days free. Each volume contributes to an impressive home library, certain to become a treasured family heirloom...to be enjoyed again and again.

Mail the card at right today.

Now in handsome Heritage Editions

Each matching 6" x 9" volume in The Collection is bound in rich Sierra-brown leatherette, with padded covers and embossed gold title... creating an enduring family library of distinction.

angry red of the morning sky. The Cheyenne boy waited, straight and proud as a buffalo lance, for the great warrior to continue.

What happened next is still told with high tribal pride upon the Montana and Wyoming reservations.

"We may not meet again," said Little Wolf. The words and the stern look were for Red Bird. "Your way lies with your grandfather, for he is old and needs you at his side. You will go with him, abiding always by his counsel. Do not leave him, do not fail him. He is the last real chief of our people."

He turned to Dull Knife, placing his slim hand on the old chief's shoulder. "Peace, father. May Maheo ride with you." Then, quickly, to Red Bird. "And you, Maevess-onsz," he made rare use of the diminutive 'little red bird,' "you put your arrow at my feet when you thought I sat alone. See now!" he concluded with fierce pride, holding up his beautifully engraved Winchester, "I do as much for you!"

With the words, he stooped and placed the priceless rifle on the ground at Red Bird's feet. At once he stepped back, drew himself up, touched his brow toward the speechless Cheyenne boy. *"Enitoeme,"* he murmured softly, and swung on his heel and went away.

He did not look back. When he had passed from sight behind the farther lodges, Red Bird saw him no more. For the boy, as for history and the 148 of his tribesmen who would follow Dull Knife along the white man's road, it was the same.

Hokom-xaaxceta had said his savage farewell.

The War Chief was gone.

The last mark on Weston's map was the Lohburg ranch. He checked it again now for the hundredth aimless time since bringing the rancher's widow and children into the fort. He shook his head hopelessly. Getting up from his desk he tore another leaf from the wall calendar, noted the date, the 20th, sat down again, began to reshuffle the stack of telegraph messages piled before him.

At the moment, Crook still had five field columns activated between Lincoln and Laramie, east and west, and Ogallala and Robinson, north and south. The Cheyenne were still somewhere within the perimeter of a hundred-mile circle compassed upon their last known location—the Lohburg ranch, and were still, despite that narrow pinpointing, as lost to the army as though they had a million miles in which to maneuver.

The top-of-the-pile communiqué, the one Corporal Feeney had brought over the night before, and which had kept Weston awake to the present daylight, was the one currently putting the C.O.'s fingers to drumming his desktop.

It was from Crook and announced bluntly that the Cheyenne were sealed off south, east and west, had only one way left to go—Weston's way. Crook further reprimanded the Robinson commander for his failure to locate the Indians within the past week, and closed with the insistence this failure be at once rectified by putting every available man into the field within twenty-four hours. It was an order, leaving no way out. Not to comply with it would mean loss of command and a military board of inquiry.

Weston had delayed going out after the Cheyenne for a personal, albeit very awkward military, reason—Amy Lohburg.

The ranch woman had made a profound impression on Fort Robinson's lonely commander. That impression had not lessened after the junior officers' wives had given her a fresh set of settlement clothes and, as they condescendingly put it, "fixed the poor thing up." In turn, Amy had found much in the dignified manner of the post's middle-aged C.O. to contrast favorably with the undisguised oglings of the younger officers. In view of the mutual feeling Weston had listened sympathetically to the ranch woman's insistent story that Red Bird had told her the Cheyenne meant to come into Fort Robinson and surrender, providing they were left alone to do so in their own way and time. The added, emotional corollary to his decision to believe Amy's report, and to give the Indians their chance to come in peaceably, was the fact they still held captive the brave girl's small son, Billy.

His hesitant stating of these official and humane reasons to headquarters at Laramie was what had drawn the stinging rebuke he now studied. Nor, worse yet, did his troubles end with Crook's displeasure.

His own staff and command, keyed up by the restless Jackson, were overripe for action, were angrily calling in officers' quarters and enlisted barracks alike, the obvious questions on their new C.O.'s courage. In the literal, if crude comment of First Sergeant John Lundy, "morale at Robinson was worser off than a wet dog with no place to shake."

Under the circumstances, the last officer Weston wanted to see that early morning of October 20 was Captain J. T. Jackson. Nevertheless, glancing out the office window now, a man had to admit that the tall young cavalryman hurrying across the frozen parade ground bore a disturbing resemblance to his eager second-in-command. The bearded, buckskinned figure accompanying him did nothing to ease a bedeviled commander's conscience, either.

Alec Raynald was a six-foot, swarthy Scot whose principal employments were those of post Indian interpreter at Robinson and army ambassador-without-portfolio to the Pine Ridge Sioux. The fact he was trotting along in Jackson's wake let Weston suspect that something more than the smell of breakfast bacon was in the Fort Robinson wind.

He was right.

And the smell was a long march from pleasant.

"Well, Major," Jackson came aggressively to the point, "now we can move. Raynald has brought us what we've been waiting for. I've already ordered assembly blown." As his words were echoed by the staccato of the bugler's call blaring from the parade ground, Weston only looked at him thoughtfully. Passing over the brash assumption of command with a mild nod, he turned to the interpreter.

"Hello, Alec. What's this all about?"

"It ain't good, Major," said the big Scot earnestly. "The Sioux have got word that the Cheyenne are camped on Clear Fork down south of the Niobrara."

"Fine," smiled Weston. "That would seem to indicate that Mrs. Lohburg was right. You see, Jackson," he added happily, "sometimes it pays to be overage and move a little slow. Our Indians are coming in quietly, just like the Cheyenne boy said they would."

"I'm afraid that ain't quite the way it is, Major," apologized Raynald. "You see the old man, that's Dull Knife, he wants to come on in and give up. But that crazy Little Wolf ain't about to follow him. The way the Sioux get it he's aiming to split off with better than half the tribe and head on west for the Powder."

"Yes, *Major*," interrupted Jackson acidly. "And the way I get it is that we've no choice but to jump that camp before Little Wolf does. You know who will be held responsible if he gets away. I don't think I need remind you of that."

"No, that's right, Jackson, I don't think you do." Weston turned quietly back to the interpreter. "You are absolutely sure they're camped down there at Clear Fork, Alec?"

"No sir, not absolutely I ain't. All I got is the Sioux's word for it. Naturally, I ain't had time to scout down that way and make sure."

"Naturally," agreed Weston, relieved. "Jackson, I think we'll just send Alec on down the trail to look around a bit before we move any troops out." Jackson's reply would no doubt have furnished grounds for court-martial but he did not get to deliver it. The office door banged open at the same time the Captain's mouth did and Sergeant Lundy bulled in dragging a grinning, tousle-haired white boy.

"This here's the Lohburg kid, Major. A Cheyenne sprout not much bigger than him just brung him up to the main gate. The Injun kid cut and run before we could grab him but this here Lohburg boy is fuller of Cut Arm information than a buffer wallow is of bull-water. He's also," added Lundy admiringly, "fuller of guts than a guv'ment ammunition mule!"

In five minutes the half-starved white boy had told what he knew about the Cheyenne camp and was on his way, via Lundy's proud shoulder, to his mother's arms.

Unhappily for Major Weston, what Billy Lohburg knew was more than enough: the hostile camp *was* on Clear Fork, there *had* been a split between Dull Knife and Little Wolf, the latter *was* gathering his followers and preparing to strike his lodges. In the uncomfortable silence which followed the boy's departure Jackson turned on Weston.

"Well, Major," he demanded, "what do you think now?"

There was no more time to think, Weston knew that. He kept his voice down, his gray eyes steadily on his angry subordinate "Now, Captain, I think you had better prepare to leave at once. Take Troops E, F, G and H. Detach Lundy and Meeker as scouts. Give their troops to Murchison and MacCloud. Take Alec along, of course. Any questions, sir?"

"None!" snapped Jackson excitedly.

"Good. How do you propose to go?"

"A wide swing west to cut Little Wolf off from the Powder. If we miss him, close in on Dull Knife's camp."

"All right then, one last thing."

"Yes sir."

"Above all, I want this understood. If you succeed in pinning Dull Knife down without a fight, do not try to disarm him."

"Good Lord, you can't mean that!" exploded Jackson.

62

"These are *hostiles*. They've been murdering right and left ever since they crossed the Republican."

Weston looked away from him, out across the parade ground. "Jackson, you were with Crook in the Big Horns. You went in with Mackenzie when the General sent him ahead to seek out and destroy Dull Knife's village. Is that not correct?"

"I understand you were on Crook's staff," snapped the other. "You ought to know."

Weston broke his eyes from the window, brought them back to his angry junior. *"I do,"* he agreed. "I also know what Crook said to us after it was all over. *After,"* he added slowly, "we knew how many unarmed women and children you had left in the snow up there."

"Good God, Weston, that was war. When you're fighting Indians a few squaws and kids always get in the way. You just don't know!" he finished defiantly.

Certainly, Howell Weston heard him. Just as certainly he continued in his own plodding track. "Crook called all of us up to the command tent. One of Luther North's Pawnees had just brought in the news. Crook asked him to repeat the information for us. 'Gentlemen,' he then said quietly, 'let this be a lesson to you. If you ever *need* to make an Indian fight, just tell him you are going to take his gun away from him.' I've never forgotten that moment, Jackson—neither the moment nor its meaning."

"If I may say so, sir," gritted the younger officer, "you had better forget both. The situations are scarcely comparable."

"Meaning what, sir?"

"You're not Crook and you're in trouble!"

"Exactly, Jackson."

"Exactly what, for God's sake?" cried the exasperated youngster.

"What I said to begin with," repeated Weston patiently. *"Don't try to disarm those Indians."*

Jackson shook his head savagely, sat back on his flaring temper, got it under control. There was a time and a place for anger but never at the expense of ambition. Nor of nailing down military responsibility. "If that is your final decision, Major Weston," he challenged, "I'm afraid I will have to ask you to make it an official field order. In writing."

Weston sat back in his chair. Cocked his white head thoughtfully. Looked up at the stiffly braced youth. Nodded soberly. "Jackson, do you trust me?"

The sheer simplicity of it caught the latter off guard, released the quick emotion of his inherent honesty. "Certainly I trust you!" he blurted. "What's that got to do with it?"

"Everything," said Weston gently. He stood up. Moved around the desk. Offered the embarrassed officer his outstretched hand and one of his shy, awkward smiles. "There will be no written orders, Jackson," was all he said. "Good luck, boy."

CHAPTER 12

PROFESSIONALLY, Jackson was a good soldier, and Weston's reliance on him was a matter of considered judgment. He saw past the big black hat, the Custerian mustache and the aggressive temper. The boy had born in him what Weston himself could never acquire—the inherent will to kill. Either you had that natural immunity to human suffering, your own or your enemy's, or you did not. The difference was what made fighting men. And John Tenney Jackson was a fighting man.

He pushed his four troops southward down the western Nebraska line with all speed, yet with commendable caution. When he crossed the headwaters of the Niobrara twenty-four hours later without having cut any Cheyenne sign, he abandoned Little Wolf and the border, swung his command due east for Clear Fork and the Dull Knife camp.

It was not in the nature of his superb confidence to imagine that he had actually missed the War Chief's dissident band. Rather, he at once assumed he had beaten them handily to the boundary line, now had his troops solidly between them and their reported Powder River goal. To make doubly sure of the entrapment, he put Lundy and Meeker to outriding the shoulders of his advance, north and south, while sending Alec Raynald and three of his Pine Ridge Sioux scouts probing far ahead of the column in search of Dull Knife's village.

All the following day, the 22nd, he led his command eastward, cutting the upper channel of the Clear Fork an hour before sunset. Lundy and Meeker were waiting there ahead of him. They had struck the stream earlier in the day above and below his position and followed it down until they met. Neither of them had seen any sign of Little Wolf's flight, nor of Dull Knife's village.

Jackson cursed his luck, made makeshift camp, worriedly pondered his next move.

His four lieutenants were of little help. In the mind of each lay the same uneasy question. Suppose *all* the Cheyenne had decided to pull out and follow the rebellious Little Wolf? In the mind of each, as well, arose the same disturbing answer. If they had and were now on the move rather than camped up north on the Clear Fork, what chance to intercept them had five junior officers and four troops of tired cavalry, where Crook and his four thousand men had already failed to do so?

The natural focus for this unhappiness was Weston and his old-womanish delay in sending them out after the hostiles. As of full twilight in that dispirited camp of the 22nd, Major Howell K. Weston could not have won a popularity contest with an indisposed skunk. But when an hour after sunset, Alec Raynald and two of his three Sioux rode in, military business and young officer morale along the Clear Fork picked up considerably.

The third Sioux, the agency interpreter reported, was unable to come because of a previous engagement, one that Raynald had made for him about four hours ago. It was a social assignment of some distinction—watching Dull Knife's camp while Raynald and the remaining Sioux rode back to collect Captain Jackson and his stalled command.

To the excited questions of the latter, the big Scot made dour answer. He, Raynald, was pretty old at this sort of business. Old enough at it, in any event, not to go poking his white nose into a camp of High Plains hostiles in broad daylight. He and his Sioux friends had piled off their ponies the minute they had spotted cookfire smoke. They had not gotten anywhere near close enough to count cowskins and determine if Little Wolf's lodges were still with those of Dull Knife. In Raynald's opinion, however, they probably were. In his further opinion, that assumption left Captain Jackson with two moves. He could stay where he was, closing in with daylight and gambling that Little Wolf would not attempt to run and fight when he spotted the approach of the Pony Soldiers. He could move up right now, tonight, and have the camp in an airtight surround by sunrise.

The only time Jackson took with his decision was that required to jump to his feet and yell for his orderly. The column was broken out, mounted up and on the move within minutes of Raynald's return. Raynald led the way, due north along the Clear Fork. By his order, Jackson kept his troops in a long thin column of twos and moving as close to the stream as its border brush would permit. Despite the fact this route offered a stoneless, sound-free path of tree-shadowed bottom loam, the wandering course of the fork made it seem interminably slow. But when Jackson spurred impatiently forward to complain to Raynald, the latter sent him back with some disturbingly simple food for Indian thought.

"On a quiet night, Captain," advised the big Scot, "a Cheyenne can hear a shod horse hit a dry rock six miles away—upwind."

Dull Knife was the first one awake. An old man did not need much sleep and it was growing cold in the lodge. It made the kidneys ache.

He got up, shuffled outside, stirred up last night's cookfire, put on the little pot of creek ice and willow bark. The pungent tea had not yet begun to boil when the first shaft of the morning sun struck something bright on the low hill beyond the stream. He squinted narrowly, not moving his head but only his eyes. He flicked them across the water again, then to the other hills crowding the campsite north and south. Lastly he shifted them to the shadows of the eastern hills on his side of the fork. *Aii-ee!* There was no doubt now. A man could look, and look again. It made no difference.

In fifty years of peering into the prairie's sharp crystal of sunlight one learned to read the glance of a sunshaft from many things. From distant water. Glistening snow. A bright rock. Hot sand. Any number of innocent things.

And some few more deadly ones.

Like Pony Soldier rifle barrels.

Like *those particular* Pony Soldier rifle barrels. The ones which now had his camp ringed on every side. And closely enough to blow a man's bowels away without troubling to look through a Springfield sight to do so.

Dull Knife stood up very carefully. Stepped clear of the fire. Turned to the nearest guns, those in the cross-stream sunlight. Raising his voice with the swift upward reach of his arms, he spoke slowly and clearly.

"We are here in peace. My people are sick and hungry.

They welcome their soldier friends from Fort Robinson."
Then, hopefully, and as though expecting from the skill with
which it had been conducted that his old friend of happier
times had led the surround, "Where is Three Stars? Where is
General Crook? I am waiting to see you, Nahe Hotoxceo." In
the morning hush his calling of Crook's Cheyenne name
carried with echoing clarity. But it was a hundred miles to Fort
Laramie and Three Stars was still asleep. Captain John Tenney
Jackson answered him.

"Listen to me, old man, you are surrounded!" He stepped
from the creek brush into the open sunlight, announcing his
ultimatum in his stilted Cheyenne. *Naestana maatano!* Put
down your guns!"

It was the order for surrender, total and unconditional. Dull
Knife understood it as such, answered in direct kind. *"Na-
voneoz niseneo,"* he signaled, "I hear you, my friend. I submit.
I am conquered." He made the peace sign, then added with
urgent seriousness, "But do you now give me a little time to tell
it to my people. They are not fully awake. They will be
frightened when they come out and see you there."

Jackson was not inclined to push his luck but before he
could agree to the old chief's request the Cheyenne camp was
getting awake. Fully and fast. The sleepy braves came tumbling out of their lodges reaching for their stacked guns and
racing for their tethered night horses.

"Hold your warriors! Keep them away from those horses!"
yelled Jackson, forgetting his proud command of the native
tongue in his excitement but not, even then, his hard store of
nerve. "Stop them, by God, or I will begin firing at once!"

Dull Knife ran toward the lodges calling out for his followers to stop or be killed. Pleading with them to think of
their squaws and little ones. To look around on the hills and
see where the Pony Soldiers were. To count them quickly. To
add up in their empty heads how many times the sun was
flashing along those rifle barrels.

It was only by grace of his scornful sarcasm and the harsh
screaming of the squaws which supported it, plus Jackson's
good sense in shouting before shooting, that another Sand
Creek or Wounded Knee massacre was averted. As it was, a
difference of no more than a deep breath obtained between a
senseless slaughter and a peaceful surrender. But the frightened braves did stop running and not one of the nervous
troopers touched off the lethal opening shot.

Inside of ten minutes the camp was quiet and its aging leader was splashing across the Clear Fork to arrange the final conditions of his people's submission to the Pony Soldiers from Fort Robinson.

At first, things went well.

Jackson, conversing soberly with the old chief in Cheyenne, was impressed. These were different Indians than the unstable Sioux. The latter had in previous years surrendered half a dozen times, only to leave the reservation and go back to fighting or, if not placed upon one of the agency rosters, breaking the terms of their truce in the field where it was granted them. The Cheyenne on the other hand had never surrendered until their last year's agreement with Crook, and even Jackson recognized the shameful double dealing from Washington which had followed that affair and which had resulted in Dull Knife's trusting tribesmen being sent south to Oklahoma.

As he talked now with the soft-voiced leader of the northern nomads he could not help but feel the spell of his immense dignity and iron character. In quick, friendly succession the agreements were reached. Rations for the starving fugitives would be at once freighted down from Fort Robinson. While they awaited these supplies the Cheyenne would be allowed to rest where they were, Jackson's men going into camp a discreet distance across the creek. Once they were at Robinson, General Crook would be advised of the arrival and a meeting arranged between him and his old friend Dull Knife. The Indians would be permitted to enjoy the ordinary freedom of village life while on the trail to the fort.

Querying Dull Knife as to why he had not come into Robinson of his own accord the past week, Jackson was told that scouts had been sent ahead to look for the old Red Cloud Agency. They had found it abandoned and fearing this might mean some unfavorable change in command or treatment at the fort, the band's council of elders had decided to stay where they were until they might find out otherwise, or until the Pony Soldiers should discover them.

To the question of Little Wolf having been allowed to break away the old chief only shrugged and murmured, "Who bridles Hokom-xaaxceta puts a bit in the teeth of the wind." He scooped up a handful of the fine sand from the creekbank, tossed it into the air. The morning breeze caught it, whirled it

68

away. Dull Knife speared his hand into the center of the gust, as an old man will do to catch a droning fly. He extended the closed hand toward Jackson, opened it with a weary smile. "Yesterday I had him in my hand. Where is he today?"

Jackson shook his head, thinking that what could happen to one handful of Cheyenne dust might very well happen to another. Little Wolf's escape could be officially charged to Weston's account. But if this sly old rascal should decide to evaporate with the rest of the hostiles, headquarters would want to know the name and serial number of the bright young officer who had sat on his haunches in the Clear Fork sunshine and let him do it.

Adding to his uneasiness, a steady parade of warriors had been coming down from the lodges to crouch silently across the stream and watch the parley going forward between their chief and the leader of the Pony Soldiers. The fact that each of these deadpan scorekeepers had a well-oiled rifle laid across his lap did very little to increase a man's supply of self-assurance.

In the end, Jackson could not get his eyes off those rifles. Nor his mind very far away from the fact that as long as the Cheyenne still had them his service record was at the mercy of the first uneasy buck who might decide he had changed his mind about coming into Fort Robinson. And who might belatedly wish he had gone with Little Wolf in the first place.

"It is agreed then?" Dull Knife presently reminded him. "We understand one another?"

Jackson acted as though he had not heard him and Dull Knife was forced to repeat the questions. In response, he came to with a start, frowned quickly. "No, no, not quite. I'm afraid there's one other thing."

"How is that?" asked Dull Knife, looking straight at him.

"The guns. I must have the guns."

"That is a bad thing. I would not ask it, my son."

"It is a necessary thing. I must ask it."

"Do you not trust my people?"

"Do you trust mine?"

Dull Knife felt the shaft of that one. It went deep and there was no answer for it. "But we are not enemies, you and I," he delayed. "We are not at war. We have made our peace just now." Jackson shook his head. "That is not for you and me to say. You will have to talk to General Crook about that, and he to the Government in Washington. I should not need to tell you that."

"You will not change your mind then?"

"I want those guns, old man." His voice went flat. "We have talked too long. You had better tell the warriors right now."

Dull Knife regarded him searchingly. He saw that he truly meant to have the guns and that he would talk no more about it. *"Nohetto,"* he said, "let that be the end of it." He stood up, gestured across the stream to his followers. Jackson, whose mastery of the sign language was incomplete, turned to Raynald. "What's he telling them?" he rasped. "By God there had better not be any treachery here or they will get exactly what Mackenzie gave them before!"

"He's telling them to go get all the other guns out of the lodges and bring them across to us," grunted the Pine Ridge interpreter.

"Oh," Jackson was now more than a little relieved. "Well, that just goes to show you they will jump fast enough once you let them know you won't stand for any of their sneaking nonsense."

Raynald wagged his head. "Now, I reckon I wouldn't leave them hop to it so quick, providing I was you, Captain."

"What do you mean, man?" Jackson caught the note of warning. "Speak up, speak up."

"Well, I just wouldn't leave them bring *me* the guns. I'd go fetch them for myself."

"You think they might try to hide some of them out on us?"

"I don't think no such thing," grinned Raynald. "I know damn well they will."

Jackson wheeled angrily on the Cheyenne chief. "Dull Knife, tell your warriors to stop right where they are. We will come across and get the guns for ourselves. We mean to look in every lodge and do not require any help in doing it."

The time for diplomacy was past. Dull Knife knew it. He called Jackson's order sharply across the little stream. The warriors, beginning to break up and head for the lodges, stayed obediently where they were. In response to further instructions from Dull Knife they began to pile their weapons upon the creekbank, each making a great show of opening his blanket to show the watching Pony Soldiers that his body was clean and that he carried no hidden firearms upon it. As this went on, Dull Knife turned back to Jackson. "When the last gun has been put upon the sand," he told him earnestly, "we will cross over and look in all the lodges the way you have said."

On the point of being satisfied, the young officer was once more jogged by the alert Raynald. "The hell with that, Captain. We'd best get right over there. I think I seen a couple of bucks sneaking for them tipis before you had the main pack of them hold up."

That did it for Jackson. Over Dull Knife's urgent objections, he ordered the village streets cleared and each family sent into its own lodge. Then, with the troops keeping the entire camp under cocked-rifle enfilade, picked squads went through each cowskin dwelling from one end of the silent village to the other. By the time the last tipi had been ransacked Jackson would have sworn that not an ounce of powder nor a broken hammer sear remained of armament among the Cheyenne, and would have guaranteed that Raynald had been wrong and that none of the warriors had gotten into the lodges ahead of the troops.

He would have been short on both counts.

Just before the interpreter's warning to Jackson, Bull Hump and Wild Hog *had* slipped away from the creekside group and disappeared among the lodges. They stood now, arms folded, faces expressionless, watching the last of the firearms from the tipis being stacked upon the sand. Behind them, equally impassive, stood the main pack of blanketed squaws and dirty children who had followed the search squads down from the village. Dangling as innocent ornaments upon the bracelets and necklaces of those squaws, carried warmly between their naked breasts, stuffed into the cradleboards of their nursing infants, or clutched in the grubby hands of older youngsters as harmless toys and trinkets were the working parts of five rifles and eleven revolvers. Together with enough of cartridge brass, cast bullets, powder and primers, to fill a fifty pound Du Pont canister.

As Dull Knife had warned.

And Fort Robinson would find out.

It was a bad thing to try to take an Indian's gun away.

CHAPTER 13

THE CHEYENNE VILLAGE moved very slowly toward Fort
Robinson. It took the pace of the weakest squaw, the most
emaciated child. Eight days and four camps were consumed
in making forty miles. There was plenty of time for Bull
Hump's woman to think. In the darkness of the fifth camp,
with but one more day and a short eight-mile march remaining, she reached her decision.

Moxtavehoa, Black Woman, was a half sister of Little
Wolf. She was as dark of skin and mind as her moody kins-
man. With him, she shared an abidingly distrustful nature
and a wolf-shy suspicion of the white man's given word.
Crouched sleeplessly in her mate's lodge, she thought about
tomorrow and tomorrow's prospect—another agency, another
long time of little food and no freedom, another endless imprisonment by the hated Pony Soldiers.

No! She could not do it. Hokom-xaaxceta had been right.
The white man's way was not the Cheyenne's. *Nohetto,* so be
it—sometime during the black hours of that last dawn Bull
Hump's woman would disappear.

First daylight and a very worried Bull Hump brought the
news that she had done so to Dull Knife. There was reason
for the old warrior's concern over his squaw's disappearance.
This was no simple matter of a missing wife. If it were, a good
beating would settle everything. As it was, Black Woman's
flight put them all in the shadow of serious trouble. Pondering the fact, Dull Knife decided to say nothing about it to
Jackson.

It was a grave and not an easy decision. The basic agreement of any Indian surrender to the white man had always
been that the responsible native leadership would report any
missing members of his tribe. Accepted procedure then became for the white commander, or Bureau Agent, to hold tribal hostages until the absent ones might be induced to return
and give themselves up. It was a harsh but not unfair rule, the

old chief knew. There was no other practical way, short of a Springfield bullet, for the whites to control their wild charges.

Still, in this case Dull Knife was certain that Black Woman would not be missed immediately and that she would rejoin the column somewhere along the day's march. Meantime it was better that the very young Pony Soldier chief not be disturbed in his belief that everything was moving smoothly under his proud command.

The unfortunate truth was that the old chief did not like or trust Jackson, was actually afraid to say anything to him. If the new soldier chief at Fort Robinson should prove more friendly, that would be the time to mention Black Woman's disappearance. Meanwhile, the Cheyenne had a saying—*novos ehestohe hehe napoeno*—the less said the sooner mended.

Ordinarily, it was an excellent saying.

But when the hour is late and the wind in the wrong place, all signs are apt to fail. That last camp out of Fort Robinson was a bad time for Cut Arm proverbs. If Jackson's seizure of the Cheyenne rifles was the powder keg, Dull Knife's failure to report the flight of Bull Hump's woman was the fuse. All that remained to be supplied was the match.

During the following weeks and in his thoughtful paternal way Major Howell K. Weston took certain care of that.

It went well at first. Since Robinson was an army post, not an Indian Agency, there was plenty of good food and excellent quarters for its red guests. The Cheyenne were allowed unrestricted freedom to range and hunt in the surrounding hills. The only condition was that each of the tribe's males check in at the nightly warriors' mess served in one of the post's unused barracks. This simple device permitted Weston to keep absolute track of his irresponsible captives. Its foolproof basis lay in a trick so unobtrusively played upon them that Dull Knife's haughty braves never did catch on to it.

Not until that last, shameful night.

The Major's roll-call contrivance ranked in naïveté with his famous map and in the end it worked with the same devastating accuracy. He merely had the mess sergeant in charge of the Cheyenne barracks issue a numbered cup to each of the warriors. In Weston's desk drawer was a printed list of those numbers. Opposite each numbered cup was the name of the red brother who regularly gulped from it his syrupy *moxtavhop*, the white man's sugar-thickened black coffee.

As patronizingly as his chart of the hostiles' homeward march had become known about the post as "the Major's nit-wit map," his cup-numbering system was tagged "Old Mother Weston's Cheyenne Coffee Club." The cynical label stuck and C.O. stock dropped another ten points on the Northwest Nebraska Exchange.

Weston himself was unaware of the fluctuation.

To the contrary, he became intrigued with the color and wild character of his new charges, spent all his free time in their camp. In those first trouble-free weeks he proved a growing source of comfort to the Cheyenne. They liked his quiet voice and steady eyes, respected his straight talk and silver-white hair. This officer was no *onistatan emonae,* no young fool with fire in his heart and his finger on a trigger. He was *voxpemeaz,* a wise old graybeard like themselves. By the end of November the Council of Elders nodded in sober, grateful agreement. *Pavhetan.* Major Weston was a good man. *Heves enevo.* He was their friend.

Dull Knife brought the decision to Weston in person.

It was a bitter cold night. The C.O. was working late and alone in his office. He did not hear the door open, and looked up, startled, to see the old chief standing in the cross-room shadows. "We have talked long about you," said the latter softly. "We think you are our friend. We pray for you." Before Weston could answer, or think to answer, he was gone. He simply touched his brow toward him, muttered "good night" and went out the door.

The following morning, stirred by the old Cheyenne's tribute, Weston visited the Indian camp with some news he had been hesitating to divulge for fear of arousing hopes and hungers which might not, in case of eventual disappointment, be so easily appeased. But in the face of Dull Knife's trusting gesture he could no longer withhold the good tidings. He had, he told his red listeners, recently received assurances from their good friend, General Crook, that every official pressure was being brought to bear in Washington to gain permission for the Cheyenne to stay on indefinitely at Fort Robinson. Further, the chances looked very good that Three Stars would succeed in gaining the necessary Government agreement to his proposal.

The Cheyenne took the encouragement literally. That night the drums boomed around the dance fires until dawn. The celebration went forward until daylight and final exhaustion forced the last dancer to drop. It was a great dance but then it had been a great victory. The Cut Arm People had come home at last. *And Three Stars had said they could stay there.*

Under this lethal delusion conditions on the post improved notably through early December. By the time the warming spirit of Christmas began to melt down some of the professional pessimism of Weston's command, even such die-hard detractors as Sergeants Meeker and Lundy were commencing to weaken. Captain John Tenney Jackson, himself, was beginning to wonder. What the hell? Give the devil his due. And Old Lady Weston his. Perhaps, after all, the qualities of Christian light and human charity were not completely lost upon the heathen redskin.

It was a beautiful thought.

Fort Robinson was given very little time to dwell upon it.

CHAPTER 14

WESTON FELT a little self-conscious in his new bearskin coat. Made from the glossy first winter pelt of a yearling cinnamon cub, it was the artful handwork of Dull Knife's squaws. In presenting it to him the old chief had pointedly reminded him of the similar gift of the Sioux to General Nelson A. Miles. From the occasion of that earlier gift had dated Miles's Oglala name, "Bear Coat," and from it had grown the Sioux respect and trust which had made Miles to Red Cloud's folk what "Three Stars" Crook was to the Cheyenne.

Knowing this, Weston could only assume that in giving him the coat Dull Knife meant to elevate him into the rare company of Crook as a friend and defender of his people. Hence his original embarrassment at accepting the garment and his present, awkward pride in wearing it.

Crossing the parade ground he managed to return the wondering stares and belated salutes of a passing drill squad without yielding to the temptation to look back and see how the men were reacting to their first sight of the Cheyenne fur piece. Mercifully, his errand gave him no time to ponder that prospect. Halting in front of H Troop barracks he stepped toward its silent door, knocked as diffidently as though he were a new recruit and the rickety building housed no brass below brigadier.

In the moment before the weathered planks swung open he brought his thoughts into closed-company order.

He had turned over his own C.O. quarters to Amy Lohburg and her youngsters, had been bunking in the drafty harness shed which served as a BOQ for Fort Robinson. From the loneliness of these lodgings he had observed the Christmas preparations going forward in the married officers' quarters and had not missed the big-eyed attention which the ranch woman's children had been devoting to these activities. The emotional impulse now prompting him to seek out Sergeant Lundy's assistance had occurred at once. But with his peculiar ability to discipline himself where he could not require more than a proper salute from the lowest enlistment on the post, he had pushed it aside and made every busy effort to forget it. Then, with the present day's sun half an hour high and shining gloriously, he had surrendered. After all, it *was* the day before Christmas. And it *was* his official duty as Post Commander to extend the social amenities of the season to *everyone* at Robinson—even if, prevented by the press of military administration from attending to each case personally, a man had to delegate some of the minor responsibilities to a reliable subordinate.

Weston nodded to himself, satisfied with his last-minute rationalizing of a mission which might have been regarded by some as less social than sentimental. He was ready when the barracks door creaked rustily and a sleepy trooper grumblingly wanted to know who the hell did not have the common decency to let a poor squad sleep on its first day off duty in six weeks.

The young soldier broke off his complaint in mid-growl, dropped his mouth open, got it shut again, hit into the best brace he could manage while standing in an open door in his underwear in front of the post C.O.

"As you were, lad," smiled Weston. "Just send Sergeant Lundy out here, will you, please?" The embarrassed youth disappeared and a moment later Lundy, half dressed and all surprised, was stepping out, closing the door, saluting mainly to soften his early morning scowl. "Yes sir, what can I do for you, Major?"

"A bit of social work, Sergeant," replied Weston, still smiling. "I'm too busy to take care of all of it and thought you might like to lend me a hand."

Too busy doing what, thought Lundy. Looking out the parade ground window? Finger-tapping his desk top? Checking his Cheyenne Coffee Club list? Fooling around with his blessed Indian map? But he said nothing, only bobbed his head again and repeated his automatic "Yes sir?"

"I want you," said Weston, no longer smiling and in fact beginning to work up a defensive frown, "to convey my personal wishes for a pleasant holiday to Mrs. Lohburg."

Lundy winced, bit his lip, thought fast.

He was not the last man on the post to have taken note of Amy Lohburg's rawboned, resurgent good looks. Offsetting her recent history of hardship and emotional shock, her new life at Robinson had wrought a dramatic change in the ranch girl. Two months of rest plus the increasingly attentive regard of the younger bachelor officers had succeeded in reversing the aging process of the prairie years. Amy Lohburg was not, even in growing young again, a beautiful woman. But her tall figure retained the hard hips and proud breasts of youth. And her gaunt, high-cheekboned face was disturbingly suggestive. A man did not look at Amy Lohburg and think entirely in terms of the comforts of home and fireside.

Not if he was a man like Sergeant John Lundy.

"Now wait a minute, Major," he countered hopefully, "maybe I ain't the best you can do for a detail like this. Meeker's off duty today, too. He's got a good way about him. Speaks right up and all that. I reckon he'd be more what you—"

"No, it's your detail, Lundy," Weston interrupted firmly. "And here's the rest of it." Quickly, he gave the surprised sergeant his instructions. The latter, at once and honestly dismayed, tried to find words for his considerable doubts. He was still trying when Weston thanked him and strode abruptly across the parade ground.

Cursing the day, the hour and the detail, the burly noncom turned and started for Weston's former quarters. A man did not mind so much being made to go see Mrs. Lohburg. But he sure as sin objected to going as line Sergeant John Alden Lundy for temporary Major Miles Standish Weston!

By the time Lundy reached Weston's cottage the comforting fact of his visit's official formality had had a few moments to sink in and to stiffen his attitude. The brave new bearing lasted just long enough for Amy Lohburg to open the door in response to his brisk knock. And for her pretty blush and delighted smile to scatter his hurriedly composed greeting six ways from last Sunday.

"Uh, er, good morning Miz Lohburg. I, uh thought uh, well that is, I reckoned you and me——"

"Yes, Sergeant?" It did not help one blessed bit, the way those level gray eyes stared at a man with that suspended smile.

"Uh, yeah. Well. Sure is a beautiful morning, ain't it, Ma'am?"

"Lovely, Sergeant. And so very early, too——" She left it hanging on the curve of another of those quirky little smiles but this one seemed to spread more quickly and with just the possible hint of a teasing sparkle in the calm eyes above it.

Suddenly, Sergeant Lundy felt very young.

His homely face lit up and for no good reason in the world, he laughed. It was a deep, rich laugh. Quick and contagious. As natural as the man behind it. For the first time in more years than she cared to recall, Amy Lohburg heard the sound of her own voice raised in the same gay scale. "Now do come in, Sergeant Lundy!" she bubbled. "People will think we've taken leave of our senses!"

Not at all sure that he had not taken leave of his, Lundy stepped past her. As he did, the rush of the room's heated air into the outer cold swept between them, bringing to him a stirring fragrance his rough bachelorhood had never known—the exciting spring flower scent of a young woman's body in lingering, still bed-warm freshness. Lundy could suddenly neither look at her nor say anything. Fully woman enough to sense his confusion and be kind enough to help him over it, Amy smiled again.

"I was just going to get the kids up. Won't you stay and have breakfast with us, Sergeant?"

He knew he had to get out now, or flee the field in defeat. "No thank you, Miz Lohburg, ma'am," he recited from desperately retrieved memory. "I just come by on Major Weston's orders to wish you a good holiday and ask if you and the kids wouldn't like to go out and look for a Christmas tree this morning. Major's orders, like I say, ma'am," he added defensively. "He's give me a twelve-hour pass and the use of the wood sled."

"A Christmas tree!" She could scarcely have been more

78

delighted, Lundy thought happily, had she been a child herself. "Sergeant, I think that would be simply grand. And the kids will just love it." She paused, voice dropping. "We always had a tree for them at the ranch."

"I ain't had one since I was a kid, myself," said Lundy slowly. "That was down in the Injun Nation. We used a Osage orange bush and hung it with trade-beads and hunks of busted looking glass." He shook his shaggy head as though the memory was not entirely pleasant, and got abruptly back on the official track. "Seeing you was alone and all, ma'am, the Major thought a tree might be nice."

"*Nice*, Sergeant?" she answered softly, "*I think it would be wonderful!*" He was just beginning to feel more at ease with her when the look she put behind the murmured gratitude caught him helplessly in the open. In the moment's time his eyes took to meet and talk with hers, the coarse, womanless span of the service years faded and fell away for John Lundy.

"You run along and roust the kids out," he grinned excitedly, rattling it off as though they had known one another all their lives. "I'll be back in twenty minutes with the sled. Put on their warm things and bundle up good yourself. I'll get old Sam Meeker to go along and help with the team and we'll pack a lunch and stay out the whole day!"

He backed out of the door, not wanting to take his eyes off her. He started away, stumbled, fell clumsily off the low stoop. Getting up, he dusted off the snow, returned her gay laugh, strode on off into the morning sunlight. As he went, his heart was as full of sudden happiness as were his deep lungs with the tingling bite of North Nebraska's winter air.

Sergeant Sam Meeker grinned, set his boots against the dashboard. "Hang on to your hats!" he yelled, and snaked the ten-foot lash of his skinning whip expertly between the long ears of the lead team. With equal spirit he leaned forward with a whang-leather "*Hee-hahh*, git along thar!" for the straining wheelers. Not to be outdone in holiday effort, the double span of grain-sassy army mules hit into their collars and lunged down the perilous slope of the snowy ridge.

Behind them, the clumsy wood sled bounced and skittered over the breaking crust as light and dancy as the trimmest settlement sleigh. In the fragrant tumble of its hay-filled bed, Sergeant John Lundy and his borrowed family laughed ex-

79

citedly, hung on for dear life and imagined there had never been such a beautiful day or happy time.

True, a hardbitten old barracks-bachelor felt a mite peculiar surrounded by so many women. Twenty years in service had done nothing to prepare a man for such things as having tiny Cathy, Amy's youngest, clinging tightly to him. Or to ready him for such feelings as looking across the sled and seeing the other two girls hanging on to their handsome mother with similar squeals of high delight. He could far better understand and take huge pleasure in the male whoops and yells coming from the driver's box where, flanking their "Uncle Sam" Meeker, Red Bird and Billy Lohburg, inseparable companions since the Indian boy had arrived at Robinson after the Clear Fork surrender, were joyously urging the mules to yet better, breakneck effort.

Now, thought Lundy, if they could just find some kind of a half-decent tree it would be on the way to becoming the best Christmas a lonely soldier had ever given himself.

But that tree business was not so simple in sparsely wooded northwest Nebraska. Presently, however, the wilderness-wise Oklahoman spotted a straggly cedar trying to hide among a bluffside stand of birch and willow. *"Timber!"* he roared, his range bull's bellow rocking the little valley, *"column halt!"*

In unquestioning response to the order, Meeker sat the mules so hard-down on their haunches that the sled caromed up over their cruppers, tipped sideways and went on over in a skidding shower of soft snow. Happily, no one got a scratch and Meeker figured he had gotten the proceedings off on just the right note of carefree informality.

Lundy heartily agreed.

Detailing his wizened comrade to cut the tree, build a fire and get the buffalo ribs (the proud contribution of Red Bird's mother) to roasting, he ordered Red Bird to guide the children up the bluff, atop which Billy Lohburg wanted to build an "Injun snowman" in honor of his "Cheyenne brother." With that done he turned to his own plans, which were a bit devious for open discussion. And perhaps a bit dubious for ready agreement.

However, Amy was more than ready to accept his covert dare of scaling a steep knob beyond the bluff from which, in his disarming words, "they could maybe get a scandalous view of the surrounding country." The rocky height was surmounted without difficulty, the view enjoyed without incident. But the

80

way back down the treacherous slope, Lundy warned frowningly, "must be got down with considerable care." Safest thing, naturally, would be for Amy to take firm hold of his hand, follow, "powerful cautious," in his exact footsteps. The start was made in good order but disaster lay in wait.

Twenty feet from the bottom of the descent, where an abandoned beaver slide dove sharply toward the frozen creekbed, Amy's trusted guide deliberately missed his footing. He plunged over the lip of the slide and, since he ungallantly refused to free her hand, took Amy with him. They plummeted down the slope, spun across the ice of the stream, came to a stop in a cushion of powder snow against the far bank. There, whether by accident or design, Sergeant John Henry Lundy wound up with his arms full of Mrs. Amy Lohburg.

The tall blond girl lay flushed and panting from the fall. Her coat was pulled open, her slender, full-breasted form pressed lightly against him. She did not offer to move, only letting her gray eyes stare widely into his. Her lips parted glisteningly, beckoning and waiting for him to come to them.

Awkwardly, Lundy tightened his arm beneath her.

She answered willingly, her lithe body arching to meet his. Their lips touched slowly. Still holding the hungry union of the kiss, Amy Lohburg drew him down with her, deliberately and with the fiercely lazy passion of experienced certainty, into the waiting shelter of the snowbank.

CHAPTER 15

NEW YEAR'S DAY dawned still and cloudless. The air was glisteningly cold, clear as rock crystal.

As he strode toward the officers' mess for his six o'clock coffee, all was right with Major Weston's little world. The new bearskin coat fitted much better than it had a week ago. The snow underfoot had a crisper, cleaner crunch. The pink flush of the coming sun had the dingiest of Robinson's shanties recolored a cheerful rose. Sampling the January air, Weston thought the heady aroma of the freshly brewed Mocha beans issuing from the cookshack's stovepipe added the last happy touch to a perfect morning.

He was right. The smell of coffee was the last happy thing about that morning.

He had just poured the first steaming cup when Corporal Peter Feeney entered the mess, saluted, handed him a New Year's greeting from General George Crook: *final word on the disposition of the Cheyenne had just come through from Washington.*

As he read the details of that disposition, even as he reread them a second and third time, Weston shook his head. It could not be true, yet there it was, and Feeney never made mistakes.

Sherman and Sheridan had reached an understanding with the Indian Bureau. The proposal of allowing the Cheyenne to remain at Fort Robinson was inconsistent with the best interests of both departments. In the immediate sense such a course would create a dangerous situation with the eight thousand Sioux and Arapaho at Pine Ridge. In the longer view it would jeopardize the entire reservation policy. A firm Indian rule had been established at great cost. Exceptions to it could not be considered. Further arguments from the Department of the Platte were not invited, nor would they be tolerated.

The decision stood.

Crook could fume, Major Howell Weston could curse and let his coffee grow cold and feel his long-sought "last chance" melting away with the snow on Corporal Feeney's boots. Headquarters had considered. Washington had concurred. Three Stars had his orders.

The Cheyenne were going back to Oklahoma.

"Sit down, Jackson." He shoved the coffeepot and an empty cup toward the latter. "I realize it's an un-Christian hour to get a man out of bed on a day like this but I'm afraid we're in trouble. Read this."

Jackson nodded without answering. Seven o'clock New Year's morning was for sure a hell of a time to be shaken out of a whiskey-sick sleep. He reached for the message and the coffeepot at the same time—and dropped the pot.

"For God's sake what next!" he exploded. "Can't those idiots ever get together on anything!"

In one way his disappointment was like Weston's. It was honest. The minute the Cheyenne were sent back south Fort

Robinson ceased to present a military opportunity. Without such opportunity the command ambitions of a young combat officer became academic. On the other hand, without any Indians to worry about, the post command became strictly an administrative job; just the dull sort of spit-and-polish monotony cut to perfect size for a forty-year-old chunk of dead staffwood like Weston.

In the silence which followed Jackson's petulant outburst Major Howell Weston was not the only officer at Fort Robinson to feel his big chance slipping away. But in his anger over Crook's message the youthful captain's resentment struck one curious snag and hung there. What a man in Jackson's position could not begin to guess was the reason for Weston's obvious upset over news which, for him, should have been nothing short of wonderful. Furthermore, in the grip of his morning-after's unpleasantness, Jackson had no intention of *trying* to guess.

"Well, it's a lousy rotten trick, Weston, anyway you look at it," he growled. "But I'll be damned if I can see where it puts you in any trouble. With the Cheyenne gone you can just sit here and collect your silver chickens without getting out of your chair!"

Weston passed the challenge, not taking its angry bait. He was still satisfied that Jackson was all right. The boy was short on temper and long on bad language. But he was military man enough to say what he thought and in the old army game of patting the Colonel's backside such aggressive honesty was worth a barracksful of brass-kissers. "The trouble, Jackson," he explained patiently, "will come when we tell the Cheyenne they're going back."

The black coffee was getting into Jackson. He was thinking faster and seeing better. "By God, Major," he admitted, "I never thought of that."

"I should have thought far more of it myself, boy. I was wrong in ever saying anything to them in the first place. The whole thing is my fault."

"Well, I guess we can't argue that," agreed Jackson bluntly. "But where the hell does it leave us?" He banged Crook's message with the flat of his hand. "This blasted thing is an order. There's nothing either you or I can do about it now."

Weston grimaced wearily. "There's something I can do, Jackson. And I'm going to do it."

Resign? thought Jackson cynically, but shook off the happy idea and only parroted, "Yes sir?"

"I can go see Crook."

"The hell you say. You're not serious—in this snow?"

"I've already talked to Lundy about it. He's ridden it many times in winter. Says we can make it without any trouble."

"But damn it, Weston, Laramie's eighty-five miles!"

"I'm going." He stood up. "You're in command. I've told Ferris. If there's anything you want to know in detail, check with him. I'll leave in the morning, be back the 5th or 6th. I think we'll take Meeker along with us. Lundy says he knows the country even better than he does. I believe that's about it. Any questions?"

"Just one. What about the damn Indians and this crackpot order of Crook's?"

"Nothing."

"Meaning what, for God's sake?"

"What I said. Sit tight and keep your mouth shut."

"Is that all?"

"It will be enough. *For you.*"

They stood a moment eyeing each other, no question in the mind of either about the sudden change in room temperature.

"Yes sir. Good day, sir," said Captain John Tenney Jackson, and turned on his heel and went out.

"Good day, sir," Major Howell Weston called after him.

He said it quietly and not unpleasantly. But very definitely to the chilly point. In a huff, a hurry, hung-over, or whatever, young Jackson heard it and heard it right. For the third time in his brief, confusing association with Fort Robinson's soft-talking, modest C.O., he had just been told off.

Short and flat and for official certain.

"But I saw him, grandfather. Just now while the white boy and I were stalking a rabbit down in the creek bottom. There can be no mistake. He had his new coat on and the tall ser-geant and the little sergeant were with him." Red Bird paused, excitedly making the sign of the running horse with his small hands. *"Nonotovetoz!"* he cried. "They were in a real big hurry!"

Dull Knife forced a quieting smile, patted him on the shoul-der. "You are a good boy to come and tell me. But go back now with your little friend and see if you can catch the rabbit."

84

"No, grandfather, something is wrong. They were riding too fast."

"I have told you to go along, boy. *Nohetto*, forget it now. It is nothing."

Red Bird nodded, unconvinced. But the inherent Indian respect of youth for age forbade any further question. Or even concern. If his grandfather said it was all right, that was the way it was. He smiled back at the old man, touched his brow toward him, backed out of the lodge and grinned at the waiting Billy Lohburg. "Now, then," he struck his chest boastfully, "let us see if a white boy can run like a Cheyenne!"

He raced away toward the creek, skimming the crusted snow light and swift as an owl's shadow. Laughing and shouting, Billy Lohburg struggled after him. Seconds later both boys were again lost in the creek timber and the really important work of running a snowshoe hare's track. The worries of mysterious, midwinter Pony Soldier missions were for older heads. *He-hau!* Let them have them! Red Bird had a rabbit to catch.

The Cheyenne boy was right about those older heads. They were at work on the problem of Weston's disappearance five minutes after he and Billy left his grandfather's lodge.

"I don't like it," Dull Knife was saying. "Something has gone wrong."

"Aye," seconded Bull Hump. "You are right. I feel it here." He touched his breast, hunched his shoulders uneasily, looked at Lone Crow. "I agree," said the latter. "Why should he ride away like that? Without saying anything to us, his good friends?"

"He is up to something, that is why!" snarled Wild Hog, who trusted no white man and feared even Weston. "I said from the first not to put so much faith in him. He is only another Pony Soldier, don't forget that."

"Yes, and he took that bull buffalo with him. That sergeant that is as high as a tall horse's head," muttered the simple-minded Big Beaver. "I mean that one that is half Cherokee. You cannot trust a Cherokee. They will steal a blind squaw's blanket. They are worse than a Pawnee or an Osage. I knew a Cherokee once that——"

"Be quiet, emptyhead!" snapped Bull Hump. "We don't care about that sergeant. It is the Soldier Chief we are talking about. Where has he gone? What is the matter? Why did he not say goodbye to us?"

"It is a bad thing," rasped Tangled Hair, the lantern-jawed, humorless leader of the Dog Soldiers. "I think Little Chief had better bring out the pipe."

"Aye, aye, the pipe!" chorused the others. "Let the pipe decide."

"Yes," said Dull Knife to the medicine man, "maybe nothing is wrong after all. Maybe we are being old women. See what the smoke says, Zcehevo."

Little Chief produced the pipe, packed it with red willow shag, took a coal from the fire, and tamped it into the carved stone bowl. He smoked for five minutes. Not a chief moved, not one took his eyes away from the upward draft of the pungent bark. At last Little Chief made the terminal sign to Maheo and Dull Knife spoke at once.

"Well, my brother, what is in the smoke this time? What does it tell you?"

The Keeper of the Arrows shook his grizzled head. "It is as you first said," he told him. "Something is wrong."

"What is to be done?" asked the old chief anxiously. "What does the pipe say to do?"

"It says to look out. To be careful. To wait a little while yet."

"How long does it say to wait?" demanded the restless Bull Hump.

"One sleep."

"And then?" It was Dull Knife again, his eyes crowfooting into narrowed pouches with the question.

"Go ask the young Soldier Chief."

Dull Knife frowned. "Does the pipe say that?" he inquired suspiciously.

"It never lies," replied Little Chief sharply. "I saw the young Soldier Chief's face in that smoke. It was there all the time grinning at me."

"How did it grin?" asked Dull Knife.

"He was happy," answered the other, *"but not for us."*

The silence held for the time it took Little Chief to knock the live dottle out of the pipe into the palm of his hand, then to powder it slowly between his fingers into the fire. And for the time it took Dull Knife to stand up and straighten his bowed shoulders.

"Nohetto," he said hopelessly. "I will go and see him in the morning."

Captain Jackson was not inclined to be so early afoot as Major Weston. His disposition, stiff-bristled at any hour, was rough as a two-day beard when official business got between him and his breakfast. He kept the Cheyenne delegation waiting a full hour and until he had bathed, trimmed his mustache, had his stack of buckwheats and started on his second cheroot. Only then did he growl at Lieutenant Ferris to "see what the s.o.b.'s want!"

The latter already had that information. He imparted it with an early morning ire as dyspeptic as his senior's.

"They want to know where Weston's gone. They wouldn't take 'none of your business' for an answer and insisted on seeing you." He paused, palming his hands helplessly. "What the hell do you want me to do with them?"

"I don't know, damn it. You might as well send them on in. They'll just sit there all day if you don't."

"All right." He hesitated again, asked uninterestedly, "What are you going to tell them?"

"The truth. What else?"

Ferris shrugged. "The Major sure won't like it. He told me to keep quiet about that order of Crook's until he got back. He even called Feeney in and warned him to shut up around the men. Didn't he say anything to you?"

Jackson stared him down. "He did," he said quietly. "He told me I was in command here."

"Yes sir." Ferris winced and saluted. "I'll send them right in, sir."

He opened the door and held it while Dull Knife and his nine subchiefs filed into Weston's inner office. When the last of them had passed him, Jackson gestured for Ferris to close the door—with himself on the far side of it. A service-wise career man, Captain J. T. Jackson. The fewer official witnesses to important and potentially questionable command decisions the better. What a fellow officer had not seen or heard he could not subsequently testify to. As for the word of an Indian, the army board of inquiry which would admit such evidence had yet to be impaneled.

Five minutes after their aged leader had put the opening, worried question to the 'young Soldier Chief,' the Cheyenne were back on Lieutenant Ferris's side of the door. In as many seconds they had been impolitely herded out upon the snow of the headquarters stoop and bid a brisk good day. Yet, stunned and bewildered as they were, they could not say they had not gotten what they came for.

The Grandfather in Washington had ordered them back to Oklahoma. Their old friend Three Stars had failed them. Their new friend Major Weston had ridden down to Fort Laramie to speak with him one last time. There was little hope to be held for the success of his mission. And worse. He would be gone many days. While he was and as long as he was, their fate would be in the unfriendly hands of the angry hearted young captain.

Havsevestoz zenxohaoo. It was a time of bad luck and blackening weather for Dull Knife's lonely people.

CHAPTER 16

ALL THAT DAY Bull Hump sat alone in Big Beaver's lodge. The latter was his true friend and had said for him to stay there as long as he liked. He had not pitched his own lodge since his woman had gone. What good was a lodge without a woman in it? What good was anything without a woman to share it? Looking in on him, Big Beaver's wife went quickly away. "Leave him alone," she told the other squaws. "Do not bother Bull Hump," she warned the children. "His heart is bad, he is thinking of his woman."

Bull Hump was thinking of his woman. And of many other things. But mostly of the harsh words of the young captain. Of what he had told them short hours ago. Of the bad news from Washington and of the shameful way Three Stars had failed his Cheyenne brothers. And of the heat and the flies and the bad meat and the sickness down there in Oklahoma.

When he thought about those things his belly felt empty within him and he was afraid. The fear made him think of his woman again. That made him lonely. When he was lonely he thought of the War Chief and of all his old friends who had gone away with him. Of how they were free out there toward the sun, and of how very happy Black Woman must be to be with them out there where the snow was clean and wide and you could ride all day and see no Pony Soldier tracks upon it.

He thought for a little while of Big Beaver and Blacksmith and Wild Hog and Noisy Walking, up there among the hills of the fort hunting that bunch of fat cow elk Blacksmith had located, and of how they had wanted him to go along and track for them.

But it was no good.

Who cared about fat cow elk or even about juicy yearling buffalo calf when his belly was so small with fear and loneliness?

No. It had been better drinking wind and eating dead ponies like they had done on the long march up here. When a man's belly was filled with nothing but hope and brave thoughts the way it had been before Hokom-xaaxceta went away, it felt bigger than it did now. *Enitoeme!* Salute the War Chief with the courage-word. He had been right. A warrior did not live by meat alone.

Bull Hump got up. He banked the little tipi fire with courteous care, so that its coals would be alive when Big Beaver's woman came to put the evening pot on. He brought his shield from its hiding place and unwrapped the precious bit of looking glass his good friend Agent Miles had given him at Darlington. Then, arranging his paint pots upon the floor, he put on his face markings. Working with deft, sure strokes he made the yellow ocher spots over he cheekbones, the zebra slashes of cobalt beneath them, the garish band of vermilion across the forehead.

When he was ready he stepped to the entrance flaps. The camp was deserted, the squaws not yet in from their evening firewood gathering. The men had not yet returned from their hunt in the hills; the children and old people were seeking the warmth of the lodge fires against the growing cold of the winter sunset.

Nomo nomonhes, this was the time.

The next moment Big Beaver's lodge was empty.

"Beg pardon, sir!" The mess orderly was breathing hard. Lieutenant Ferris nodded irritably. "All right, Spence. What's the matter now? The Indians complaining about the grub again?"

"It ain't the grub, Lieutenant, it's the coffee. More rightly the coffee cups, sir."

"The what!" cried Ferris exasperatedly.

"The cups, sir. We got one too many cups."

Weston's A.G. eyed him coldly. "Listen, soldier, if you're bucking for a ten-day tour on latrine you've come to the right officer. I'll give you five seconds to make sense, or get busted so far back it'll take you three hitches and a personal letter from General Sherman to make P.F.C. in bootcamp. What the hell do you think this is, the supply sergeant's shed? I ought to—" He broke off the eating-out in mid-bite. Swallowed strangely. Shoved back from his desk. Leaped to his feet. *"What the hell did you say, Spence?"*

"One of the Injun's cups, sir." He waved the empty tin for emphasis. "We come out with this one left over after we'd passed them around just now. Sergeant MacNally he said to run over here and have the Captain check it against Major Weston's list."

"Oh, no!" groaned Ferris, "that's what I thought you said. Give me the bloody thing—" He took the cup, gritted his teeth, headed bravely into the inner office.

Jackson took it unblinkingly. Almost, Ferris thought, as though he were glad to hear about it. But that could not be. In the face of Crook's relay of the order to send the Cheyenne back south a missing Indian could mean a lot of trouble. Real trouble. Especially for the poor Major. Jackson gave him little time to worry about Weston. He had the cup list out and the unclaimed number checked against it before Ferris could get the door shut.

"Aha! Just as I thought. One of teacher's little pets."

"Which one?" asked Ferris nervously.

"Bull Hump. He's one of their head men and one of the bunch who've sucked around Weston so much. Well, we'll take care of the C.O.'s coffee club right now. I'll put those red sneaks where MacNally won't have to worry about counting cups. And if I hear one word of Cheyenne backtalk, he won't even have to worry about counting Indians!"

"What are you going to do?" muttered Ferris. "Cut down on their rations?"

"Somewhat. For a starter we'll try bread and water for five days. If they don't have their missing friend back by then, they can try their bread dry. That's an order, Ferris."

"Yes sir," said the latter dubiously. "But won't that just make more of them get excited and want to jump camp?"

"I shouldn't wonder."

"Sir?"

"We'll see they have a mighty short run for the jump."

"How's that?"

"Throw every one of them in that empty B barracks. That goes for Dull Knife, right on down. Every last buck that's listed on this mess chart of Weston's."

Ferris shifted his feet, sparred uneasily. "Well, all right, if you say so. I'll have Feeney send off word to the Major right away. He should be able to get back by day after tomorrow."

"Lieutenant Ferris," Jackson was out of his chair leaning across the desk, braced knuckles showing white, "when I want Major Weston notified I'll let you know."

"But good Lord, we've *got* to notify him."

"Did I say I wasn't going to notify him, Lieutenant?"

"Well, no, but you said—"

"I said I would let you know *when* I wanted him notified."

"Yes, I know—"

"I will. Do you understand that, *Lieutenant?"*

Ferris, like Jackson, was a young man with a long eye for the shortest way up. He looked at the youthful, self-assured captain, thought briefly of the hesitant, overage major, wavered unhappily over the forced choice of futures. "Yes," he acknowledged awkwardly, "I think I do." Unexpectedly, Jackson laughed. He moved around the desk, clapped his junior on the shoulder in a rare display of friendliness. "I think you don't," he grinned. "Listen, Ferris, I'm not trying to overslaugh the Old Man. I'm trying to save his lousy command for him. What do you think would happen if we wired Crook that the Cheyenne had started jumping the post the minute Weston left?"

"I know, I know," admitted his companion defensively. "I did my best to talk him out of going. It was a fool stunt."

"It was a little better than that," said Jackson. "It was dangerously close to dereliction of duty. If we can't cover up for him he's in real trouble, and you know it."

"Yes, I guess I do."

"Certainly you do. This way we may be able to get that Indian back and everything quieted down without Laramie ever hearing about it. If we don't," he qualified soberly, "that will be the time to send word down there to Weston. Don't you agree?"

Whatever its motivation, Jackson's logic was convincing, and young Ferris was not a heavy thinker. "Yes sir," he agreed, relieved, "I do. Will you come with me or do you want me to handle it?"

"I'd better stay out of it. The Cheyenne don't like me and there's no use stirring them up any more than need be. You shouldn't have any trouble. They know what happens when one of them goes over the stockade."

Lieutenant Ferris, considerably bucked up by the sensible tone upon which the situation had leveled off, saluted gratefully and departed to put the Indians under guard. After all, Jackson was no doubt right. It was not the first time an Indian buck had jumped the reservation or the first time his fellow tribesmen had been put under arrest to guarantee his return. Just as the Captain had said, there should not be any trouble.

Well, perhaps not.

There was nothing morally wrong with Jackson's angry logic, nor his inherent honesty. Nor with young Ferris's gullibility.

But they were white men.

Trouble was a word spelled Cheyenne.

"B" barracks lay quiet in the winter moonlight. No light, nor sound, nor stir of movement came from within to indicate there might be life there. Yet there was. Fifty-nine Cheyenne men crouched motionless in the fireless cold of the long building. They did not speak or move about. Outside, the only sound was the regular crunch of the passing sentries' footsteps or the occasional low growl of disgruntled comment as one half-frozen guard passed another in the January night and paused to curse Captain John Tenney Jackson and the zero cold of northwest Nebraska.

Still, there was one small Cheyenne movement afoot.

Red Bird scuttled across the open moonlit snows behind the barracks the moment the patrolling sentry passed around the far corner. Before the next guard rounded the near corner he had jumped into the snow-filled rain barrel beneath the broken-paned rear window. When the second sentry had stomped by he raised himself quickly to the weathered sill.

"Psstt! Grandfather? Are you in there? Do you hear me? It is I, Maevess-onsz."

"Shh! be quiet, boy!" It was Tangled Hair who heard him and leaped to the window. "Don't let them see you. I will fetch your grandfather."

92

Dull knife was at the window then, his face gray and drawn in the shadowed moonlight. He looked very old and very tired, and Red Bird's heart felt sick and bad to see him now. "It is I, grandfather," he choked. "Maevess-onsz."

"Aye, I see you, boy. My little red bird—"

Red Bird heard one of the guards returning, ducked swiftly back down into the barrel. As quickly he was up out of it again. But the pause had given him time to taste the salt of his tears and to swallow it manfully. "Listen, grandfather," he whispered, "I came to see what I could do for the people. The women are all crying and the babies will not sleep. It is bad. I thought perhaps I might go after Bull Hump and bring him back for you. I am a good tracker, grandfather, you know that. Maybe I could—"

"Hush, boy." The old man shook his head. "You cannot catch him now. He has gone to find his woman who is with your uncle. They will never come back."

"But, grandfather—"

"No, no. That is enough now. They are with Hokomxaaxceta. That is the end of it. Go away, boy, the soldiers will see you. That would be bad. We must all be very careful until Major Weston comes back. He is our friend. When he comes back things will be all right with us again. You will see. He has gone to talk to Three Stars for us. So be quiet now and go away fast."

"But Major Weston may be gone a long time. You cannot starve in there like that." He dropped his whisper. "Left Hand and Lone Crow and Wild Hog and those other restless ones will become angry. Then there will be real trouble, grandfather."

Dull Knife heard him. As Little Wolf had said, the boy had a young head with an old tongue in it. He spoke the truth now and the old chief knew it. "Aye," he agreed dejectedly, "that is so. But our friend is already a full day gone. He is too far along the trail. There is nothing we can do to bring him back now."

To bring him back! The thought struck Red Bird with the wondrous force reserved to the imaginations of very small boys. The hazards a twelve-year-old might find in riding across eighty-five miles of High Plains winterland with a blizzard threatening like the one which had been building in the black skies to the north all day long, never occurred to him. "I will go and get him," he announced quietly. "I will catch up to

93

him and bring him back for you. I can take the south trail, the one the buffalo used in the old days. It is far shorter. And what is one day's start, grandfather? They are white men. *I am a Cheyenne.*"

The old man was very proud then. He had a hard time with his words. It was a good thing that another guard went by just at the moment. It gave him time to say it without softness. "All right, boy. You take my black and white stallion. He is very strong, a fine snow horse. If you get in a bad storm, give him his head. He will not circle with you." Then, fiercely, and full of the pride-in-blood. *"Enitoeme,* Red Bird!"

"Enitoeme, grandfather. Tell the others I am going. It will make their hearts good."

The old chief grunted softly, waved his understanding of the farewell. And that was the simple, Indian end of it. Seconds after the next sentry had passed, the rain barrel once again held nothing but snow.

CHAPTER 17

WESTON ARRIVED at Laramie late the afternoon of the second day, January 5, beating the blizzard by an hour. Crook saw him at once, receiving him in his famous canvas fatigue suit.

His appearance had not altered, thought Weston. There were the same gimlet eyes, the same burly-shouldered, ramrod frame, the same furious red mutton-chop whiskers. When he spoke it was apparent his manner was still as honestly modest as ever.

Throughout his fabulous career the great Indian fighter had made a passion of anonymity and self-effacement. His voice was as soft and pleasant as a woman's, his address as cordial as though he and his visitor had roomed together at the Point. Yet for all his unassuming warmth, he had a monumental dignity, past which in all the years he had been on the frontier no junior officer had been known to step. George Crook was a shy, sincere, compassionate man. But he was a general of the army. No man who served under him ever forgot that.

Answering Weston's anxious queries about the Washington order, he was as thoughtful and patient as a headmaster with a willing but backward pupil. "Yes, Major," he agreed, "the Cheyenne are a splendid people. They've made a bully good fight of it and ought by any Christian standards to be allowed to stay up here. But," he explained with an expressive gesture of his big hands, "Sherman and Sheridan are adamant. I myself am helpless to do more. I'm already too far out on the limb as it is. I'm beginning to hear wood crack, Weston." He paused, nodding his cocked head in that quick, bird-bright way he had. "I have made a final protest to the decision, of course. Still, that's only a part of putting myself officially on record. Nothing whatever can be expected to come of it. Like my old friend Dull Knife would say—*nohetto*, there's the end to it. The Cheyenne are going back, Weston. There's absolutely nothing we can do to alter that fact."

In reply to his listener's urgent request for a humane delay of the return journey, at least until spring might provide more clement weather, he wagged his red whiskers vigorously. "Impossible, sir. Sherman is determined to make an example of Dull Knife. I've been unable to talk him into so much as a ten-day delay. He says they got up here by themselves, let them get back the same way and as best they can."

"But good Lord, sir! They can't stand another march right now, winter or no winter!"

"They will have to," said Crook bluntly. "I've done all I humanly can for them." His pale blue eyes hardened. "Of course the main trouble is those killings they began the last few days beyond Frenchman's Fork. The public is aroused more than at any time since the Southern Cheyenne raids in 'sixty-six and 'sixty-eight. Pressure is on everybody in Washington from the Secretary of War to the last file clerk in the Indian Bureau." He cocked his head again, concluding with a final sharp nod. "If you ever get to be a general officer, Weston, you will come to know that in this man's army public opinion is your real Chief of Staff."

They talked for another ten minutes, Crook firmly answering each of Weston's hopeful suggestions for the Cheyenne with an unqualified no. In the end Robinson's harried commander knew they had come down to the bare bone of the matter: how best and most safely to break the bad news to Dull Knife and his touchy band.

Crook was kind about it but typically direct.

"Major, you should not have left your command to come down here. I don't believe I need remind you of that. I do appreciate your reasons and certainly share your emotions. I do not appreciate, nor do I share," he added quietly, "your professional opinion of Captain Jackson and your reliance upon him in this case. He was put up for the command at Robinson the same time you were. It was I who turned him down. He is an excellent combat officer, given close supervision. But he has a bad habit of enlarging on his orders and is notably a poor hand with Indians. My advice to you, sir, would be to get out of here in the morning and back up there where you belong just about as fast as a fresh horse can carry you."

In response to Weston's halting apologies, he waved his hand in embarrassed objection. "Good heavens, man, you don't have to explain how you feel. Not to me—not about Indians. I think they're the most remarkable people in the world. The highest compliment I ever received was when this same Dull Knife thanked me for looking after the Cheyenne when they were at Robinson in 'seventy-seven. He told me I was more of an Indian than he was. And he meant it."

He looked at Weston a moment, shook his head once more. "But they are children, lad. You must always remember that. Wonderful, brave, generous people, it is true. But with the hearts and minds and outrageously sensitive feelings of little children. Bear that in mind and you will always be a brother to them."

He concluded swiftly, accenting his last points with little chopping gestures of his open hands. "When an Indian is good you must never fail to praise him. When he is bad you have also got to punish him with the same speed. *Never* forget that part of it."

Weston knew they were at the end of it. He stood up, saluting gratefully. "I won't, General," he promised. "And I want to thank you for your time and understanding. I guess I don't need to tell you what that chance in command up there means to me."

"I remember you quite favorably from 'seventy-six, Major. Your staff work for me at that time was excellent. Subsequently, General Sheridan has spoken very highly of you and, as you know, General Sherman confirmed his recommendation of you. *They* seem to have a lot of faith in you, sir."

In a pretty pointed way the terse comment left much unsaid. But under the circumstances Weston felt he was lucky to be getting off with nothing more than a lecture on how to handle Indians, together with the brief advice to get back on the job of doing so. He saluted again and started out. The office door burst open before he reached it.

"Beg pardon, General," the orderly saluted sharply, handed the message to Crook, "this just came in from Captain Jackson up to Fort Robinson."

Crook read it through while Weston stood paralyzed in his tracks. When he had finished he said nothing, only passing the sheet across the desk to Weston. The latter moved forward, took it from him. He read it, put it back on the desk, stood dazed and speechless—with ominous reason.

Bull Hump was gone and Jackson had the Cheyenne under barracks arrest. They were on rations of bread and water. Their temper was bad, growing rapidly worse. The Captain Commanding at Fort Robinson respectfully requested emergency instructions from General Crook and Major Howell Weston.

Crook let his visitor stand a long time, studying him in his gentle, distant way. Finally he bobbed his whiskers, spoke very slowly. "I told you I thought you had better leave in the morning?" he reminded him quietly. Weston nodded, unable to speak. "Well, sir, I've just one small suggestion to add to that."

"Yes sir," Weston managed weakly.

"Better make it tonight," said Crook. And got up and walked around him and out of the room.

Lundy knew that trail as well as he knew the path to the company latrine. But even an outhouse can be hard to find in a High Plains blizzard, even in a fairly mild one such as he and Weston and Sam Meeker were presently bucking back up toward Fort Robinson. Somewhere after midnight he began to worry. Meeker, supposedly an older Indian country hand than himself, was equally confused and could offer no more help than to agree it was a good time to start wondering where they were.

Weston's pocket compass, consulted a short time later when the two sergeants grudgingly admitted they were lost, showed they had veered far south of their course. Beyond that they knew nothing save that the wind was rising and the temperature dropping. Turning north they rode at a walk, checking the compass every few minutes to insure against the fatal "big circle" drift common to snowstorm castaways.

It was necessarily slow work. By 2 A.M. they had covered only five miles, and still had not cut the main trail. A little farther along, the needle began to swing to the right and they knew they were losing course once more. At this point they blundered into a sheltering stand of cottonwoods and Weston called the halt. They had matches. Here were firewood and a fine windbreak. It was time to think more of getting through the night than of getting back to Fort Robinson.

They tied the horses, built a fire, huddled to it in bone-cold misery. None of them heard or saw the shadowy rider who loomed out of the storm moments after their own arrival. But if the white man's God had been busy elsewhere, the Cheyenne's had not. The fire had been laid and lit to Maheo's order—right under the freezing nose of the passing Red Bird —and not fifty paces off the old Indian buffalo trail to Fort Laramie.

Had Dull Knife's spotted studhorse not winded Weston's mare, the Indian boy would have ridden right past his lost white friends. But the stud had stopped and whickered, arousing his sleepy rider. The faint glow of the fire through the eddying snow had done the rest.

The Cheyenne youth slid off his halted pony, stalked into the guttering firelight. *"Hau, niseneo,"* he announced calmly, "it is a bad night."

Lundy jumped up and hugged him until his small ribs cracked. "That is enough now, Big Bear!" the laughing youngster gasped with dry Indian humor. "Don't kill me just yet. I might still be of some use to you."

Meeker and Weston joined in the joyous greeting, thumping him on the back, repeatedly asking him if he was all right, insisting he bundle up in the latter's bearskin coat while Lundy broke out the messkits and got the snow melting for the coffee. It was a mute tribute to their rapidly growing respect for the resources of the Plains Indian that none of the three white men thought to ask Red Bird if he, too, were lost. They simply assumed that being an Indian, he could not be.

They assumed right.

Beyond a frostbitten nose and cold-numbed hands and feet, the Cheyenne boy was as happily at home as though on a daylight summer march up his native Powder River valley. They understood this as soon as they quit fussing over him and gave him a chance to say something.

"Well," he told them in his careful schoolboy English, "you are lucky I found you. You were going in a pretty bad direction."

"Chief," grinned Lundy, patting him with mother-grizzly tenderness, "tell us something we don't know. We're lost as Bopeep's pet sheep. Whereaways is the cussed trail anyhow?"

"Well, the white man's trail is up there," he pointed northward into the snow's blindness, "half a day's ride, maybe more." With pardonable Indian pride and a superior jerk of his small thumb over his shoulder, he added, "The Cheyenne trail is right there past those trees. I could spit into it for you but the wind is against me just now."

Quickly, the talk came to its inevitable point. In reply to Weston's anxious question about conditions on the post, Red Bird lost his bright grin. "My grandfather sent me to find you, Evoxpohess." He used the Cheyenne nickname, "White Hair," by which, among themselves the past happy weeks, Dull Knife's followers had affectionately begun to call Weston. "The young Soldier Chief has put all our warriors and old men into prison up there. He did it because Bull Hump ran away. But my grandfather says that Bull Hump has gone to find his woman out there with Little Wolf and will not come back. So he says there will be big trouble if you don't come at once and let the warriors out."

"Where's your trouble in that, boy?" Lundy broke in frowningly. "Them Injuns," he used the word as though he did not regard Red Bird as an Indian, "know damn well they'll get jailed if one of them jumps camp."

"It is not just that," said the boy quickly. "The young Soldier Chief told them that Three Stars said we must all go back to Oklahoma again. That is why Bull Hump ran away."

"God Awmighty!" breathed Lundy. Then, flatly deliberate, "*That son of a bitch.*"

Weston said nothing. He was thinking of Crook and what he had said about Jackson, thinking of where he, Weston, now was, and of the last thin chance remaining to him of saving his command at Robinson. Either he got back to the post in time to prevent a repetition of the Oklahoma outbreak, or he did not. It was that simple. And it all turned on a twelve-year-old Indian boy who had already ridden thirty-six hours without sleep.

99

"Red Bird," he asked at last, "can you follow the Cheyenne trail in all this snow?"

"It is an old buffalo track," shrugged the youth. "Worn very deep and going where the snow is light. It will not fill up for a long time."

"How quickly can it take us to Fort Robinson?"

Red Bird squinted into the fire.

"If we kill the horses?" he asked presently.

"If we kill the horses," said Weston.

"And start now?"

"Right now."

"Well, by the time the sun goes down again, then. But the horses will be dead."

"He-hau!" grinned the irrepressible Lundy. "How about us?"

"You will be all right," said Red Bird unsmilingly. "Am I not leading you?"

"Nohetto!" shouted Lundy delightedly. "By cripes, there's the mother-loving end to it!" Then, cheerfully, and juggling the steaming mess pan free of the fire, "Coffee's boiled, boys. Break out your tins and dip in. She's eighteen hours to the next cup!"

CHAPTER 18

RED BIRD's cruel estimate proved exact. As they topped the last rise south of Fort Robinson the setting sun broke momentarily through the snow-haze. Lundy's horse lay dead five miles back along the trail. Meeker's mount, carrying both sergeants, lasted halfway down the final slope. Then, it too, staggered and went down. Only Weston's mare and Red Bird's stud lived long enough to bear their frozen riders past the main gate sentries. Of these the mare was dead within the hour, the windbroken little stallion slaughtered for camp-meat that same night by the Cheyenne squaws.

Weston, defying Surgeon Cummings's order to "get straight to bed with a pint of Old Crow and a mustard plaster," went at once to see the Cheyenne. He said nothing to Jackson about the latter's twenty-four-hour delay in telegraphing Crook nor about his failure to mention in that telegram his own culpability in telling the Indians of the headquarters directive returning them to Oklahoma. These were matters which could wait until Cummings's "pint and plaster" had had a chance to draw some of the poison out of a man's anger and exhaustion.

He found Dull Knife's braves huddled miserably in one corner of the barracks seeking the only warmth available to them, that of their own bodies. The moment they got the glare of the hurricane lantern borne by the accompanying Lundy out of their eyes and were able to recognize Weston, they came to their feet with a single glad cry.

"Enitoeme! Maheo be praised! It is Evoxpohess!"

Their good friend "White Hair" had come back to them, they excitedly told one another. Now they would hear something. Now they would get the real truth. Now they would have old Three Stars' answer to that terrible lie the young Soldier Chief had told them. "We are glad to see you," said Dull Knife with heartfelt simplicty. "We knew Red Bird would find you. We knew you would come back and let us out. We knew you would not fail us."

Weston held up his hand, shaking his head slowly.

Instantly, the cries of relief and the happy greeting-words fell away. The welcoming smiles froze. The gaunt faces went blank. From birth they had been taught to read sign, whether left upon the face of a trail by the passing of an animal or upon the face of a man by the passing of a thought. Upon White Hair's face now, they read a very bad sign. Their stillness became a living, breathing thing.

Weston knew it was no time for a speech. The hardest man in the world to talk around was the simple man. These were very simple men. "I'm sorry, my friends," he admitted humbly, "but I have been to Three Stars and I have failed you. What Captain Jackson told you is the truth. You must go back to Oklahoma. Washington has ordered it and there is nothing General Crook or I can do for you now."

The Cheyenne held their utter silence. There was not a sound or the flicker of a face muscle among them. They stood and looked at him, their impassive stares more accusing than any outcry. Then, quietly, they began to turn their backs to him. Within seconds the only Cheyenne in Fort Robinson's B barracks still facing him was the motionless Dull Knife.

The old chief stepped forward holding his voice purposely low. "You had better go now," he warned. "Let me talk to them. Perhaps in the morning their hearts will be better for you." Again Weston sensed the moment for keeping still. "All right," he agreed, "we will talk in the morning. Meantime, I'll have some hot food brought in for you and order a stove set up. I can't have the lot of you coming down with pneumonia."

"Just the food, my brother," corrected Dull Knife quickly. *"Never mind the stove."*

"But good Lord, man, it's freezing in here! What in the world are you thinking of?"

"I am thinking of this building," replied the old man. "It has been here a long time. The wood is very dry." Seeing Weston's puzzlement, Lundy muttered the interpretation for him. "He means B barracks would make a hell of a bonfire, Major. He don't want his little friends given no matches to play with." Weston's eyes widened. He put a hand out impulsively toward Dull Knife. "Thank you," he said, and knew from the gruff way the old man took his hand that he understood. *"Hova-hestovhan,"* shrugged Dull Knife, "it is nothing." Then, smiling wistfully as a child, *"You are my friend."*

Weston turned away. At the door he paused, squinting back across the shifting rays of Lundy's lantern. It was in his mind to plead with the Cheyenne patriarch, to argue for and insist upon some kind of definite agreement of mutual trust against tomorrow's talk. But even with the thought he was peering into the shadows behind the Indian leader.

After that there was nothing to do but go on out of the barracks, shutting the door very softly as you went. The old chief could take your hand and tell you to forget it. He could smile and say he was your friend. He could promise you he would talk to his angry braves and try to make their hearts better for you by the next day. It was no good. You looked past him and you saw those others standing there in the shadows behind him—not moving, not making a sound, not seeming even to breathe—and you had your answer.

Dull Knife's people had turned their backs on you.

Through sheer exhaustion, Weston slept. But with six o'clock and first daylight he was in the officers' mess having his black coffee on schedule. It was a crackling cold morning and was going to be clear, the storm having backed off up north during the night to growl around a little and make up its mind whether or not to take a second wind and blow up a real *zexoeto sanistove*—a real blizzard.

Meanwhile, Robinson's C.O. felt better. Ten hours of dreamless sleep and three cups of hot coffee did that for a man. The sullen behavior of Dull Knife's braves seemed less threatening now, the parting promise of their chief to talk to them more hopeful. After all, what choice did the Cheyenne have? This was not Oklahoma and the gentle Indian summer of the Middle Arkansas prairie. This was northwest Nebraska and the snow-packed cold of a High Plains winter. There was absolutely nothing they could do, no place they could go.

About now a man could forgive Captain Jackson's recent sins and thank him instead for his original toughness in seizing the Cheyennes' firearms and in subsequently insisting they be deprived of all their ponies save a dozen scrubby mounts for hunting in the nearby hills. True, you could in one way blame him for bringing the present crisis on. But in the same thought you knew that it would have come anyway and that you might not have handled it as well as he had. You would very likely have lost a lot more Indians than Bull Hump and been in much hotter headquarters' water than you were. No, actually you had to thank Jackson. And be very glad you had him in your command. Crook to the contrary, your own opinion of the boy still held. Captain J. T. Jackson would definitely do to ride Fort Robinson's roughening trail with.

Shortly Alec Raynald came in, breaking his easing thoughts. "Morning, Major. You wanted to see me?"

"Yes, Alec. Dull Knife promised to talk to me again this morning and I want you there. Lundy does pretty well with them but this time I want to be absolutely sure they all understand what is going on. With you informing the others precisely what is being said while the old chief and I talk, we should get a better feeling all the way around. Do you agree with that?"

"Could be, Major." The big Scot's shrug was not encouraging. Weston frowned quickly. "What's the matter, Alec? You know these people. You ought to be able to predict how they'll behave." Raynald grinned, shrugged again. "You're half right anyhow, Major." He did not offer to add anything to the cryptic admission and Weston had to prompt him.

"How's that, sir?"

"I know 'em."

"Well?"

"Nobody can tell you what they'll do."

"I see. Then you think we're still a long ways from being out of the woods, is that it?"

"So far from it I cain't begin to see the first break in the trees, Major. An Injun don't know himself what he'll do five minutes before he does it."

"Do you think it will do any good to talk to them again in that case?"

"It cain't do no great harm."

Weston downed his coffee. "All right, Alec, let's go. I've got a hunch they'll see things differently this morning."

"I've got a hunch you're right," said the Pine Ridge interpreter, and Weston did not like the way he said it.

Sam Meeker had the barracks guard detail that morning of the 6th. He saluted as Weston and Raynald came up. "Glad you're here, Major. I just sent a man over to get you. Our friends in yonder ain't happy."

In response to Weston's agitated inquiry, Meeker reported that the Cheyenne had refused their breakfast. They had smashed dishes, hurled mess cups through the windows, roughed up the troopers who had taken the food in. The guard detail had had to use rifle butts to get the men out without serious injury. In Sergeant Sam Meeker's hardbitten opinion there was a tidy little red prison riot building up in Fort Robinson's B barracks.

Ordering the door guards to unpadlock the building, Weston prepared to enter. As the door scraped open Dull Knife appeared, barring the way. "Don't come in," he warned blank-faced. "Go away, Evoxpohess. Go away' quick."

The change in the old man since the night before was frightening. No sign of welcome showed in the empty stare he gave the startled white officer. He stood in the open doorway, an expressionless block of gaunt red granite. His attitude was as menacing as his words. Understandably, Weston hesitated. Dull Knife repeated his warning, low voiced. "Shut the door, Evoxpohess. Put the lock back on it and go away. It is too late for talk now."

Weston stood his ground. "What should we do, Alec?" he asked his companion, but before Raynald could answer the other Cheyenne began to move up behind their leader. There were no formed words to the sound they made as they came forward. None were needed. The translation of that animal throat-noise did not require an interpreter. "We look, we listen, and we back out *slow!*" muttered the Pine Ridge man. He was not watching Weston as he spoke. His eyes were too busy with the braves behind Dull Knife. And luckily so. He saw the little ripple of movement in their front ranks before it broke into wild action.

"Watch it!" he yelled, and leaped past Weston.

His shoulder caught the latter, spinning him out of the way. The next moment he had slammed the door, banged its hasp in place, pinioned it there with the blade of his belt knife. With his broad back set against the rocking planks of the barracks door and with the enraged shouts of the frustrated Cheyenne beyond it rising in mounting fury, he grinned at the white-faced Meeker. "All right, Sarge, the knife will hold it till your boys get their kidneys unpuckered and pick up the padlock."

The lock was replaced and the commotion within beginning to subside when Captain Jackson, accompanied by the trooper Meeker had sent after Weston, hurried up. "Now what the hell?" he demanded, addressing his anger at Meeker and as though Weston were still in Fort Laramie. "Didn't I tell you not to try to go in there with less than a full squad?"

"Yes sir, you did," the little sergeant saluted unhappily. "But Major's orders, sir."

"Well?" He wheeled on Weston as though he, too, were wearing chevrons.

Still shaken, the C.O. filled him in on what had happened. Typically, he chose to make nothing of his junior's blatant arrogance. It was too late in the morning for worrying about rank-due respect. He needed Jackson now and they both knew it.

"All right," the tall youth rasped when he had finished, "I warned you not to feed them last night. But you *would* do it. Now we've no choice but to get tough with them."

Weston winced, not wanting to ask him what he meant by *tough.* "I don't think so, Jackson. I still feel they will talk. They're angry with me but I can understand that. They expected me to get somewhere with Crook and the way they look at it I failed them. I believe they'll talk to Raynald though. They know him and trust him. Alec—"

"Here."

"See if they won't let you come in. Tell them they must listen now or go without food again."

"My God!" it was Jackson again, still on the rolling boil.

"They've already thrown their damn food out. What more do you want?"

"I want to be absolutely sure they understand us, Jackson, that's all. Go ahead, Alec."

The big interpreter bobbed his head, walked slowly up to the nearest window. Making the peace sign and calling on Maheo to bear him witness that he spoke with a straight tongue he repeated Weston's plea in Cheyenne. His answer was a shatter of flying glass and a wildly thrown mess cup together with some ugly-voiced advice from Tangled Hair, Wild Hog and Lone Crow.

He listened carefully to what the three subchiefs had to say, turned and walked back to Weston. "Well, there's your answer, Major. Like I said, you can know 'em but you cain't know 'em *much.*"

"Well, well, what did they say, man!" Misled by the interpreter's wry grin, Weston asked it hopefully.

"Hell," shrugged the other laconically, "they was plumb cordial. Said if I felt like coming in, by all means to just up and do so. Allowed they'd all be mighty glad to have me join 'em and set a spell."

"Is that all?" queried Weston, belatedly wary.

"Just about," offered the big Scot, still grinning.

"Well sir!"

Raynald lost his grin, let it come hard-eyed.

"They said they'd kill me if I tried it. And, Major—"

"Yes, yes, man!"

"*They would.*"

CHAPTER 19

WESTON FLINCHED. He turned away from Raynald and stared across the empty parade ground. Presently, he moved off a few steps. "Jackson," he called, "will you come over here, please.

"A moment ago," he continued when the latter had joined him, "you said that we would have to get tough with them now. What did you mean?"

The blond youth's mouth straightened. "Major," he answered, "are you asking me what I would do if I were in your place?"

Weston returned his stare, knowing as well as his questioner where the quiet demand placed both of them, and what, exactly, they were bargaining over. The command at Fort Robinson had just been put on the block. Major Howell Weston had put it there. Captain J. T. Jackson was bidding on it.

"I am," he said.

Jackson's blue eyes flashed. Yet there was nothing either of disdain or overlording triumph in his reply but only the brittle snap of the veteran combat officer issuing field orders in the face of a suddenly and dangerously shifted tactical situation. "All right, here it is. Board up the windows. Put a twenty-four-hour chain-guard around the barracks. Round up every Cheyenne on the post—squaws, kids, babies, the lot of them—and throw them in with the men. The minute the padlock clicks, they don't get another crust of bread or drop of water until they cave in. That," he concluded flatly, "is what I mean by getting tough, *Major Weston.*"

Again Weston stared across the parade ground. All the humane doubts natural to a gentle, sensitive man hammered at his tired mind, demanding reasonable, charitable answers. But reason had failed. Dull Knife had tried it the night before. His braves had answered him by throwing their breakfast on the ground and beating the soldiers who had brought it to them. Charity had been hurled out the barracks window with the angry cup aimed at Alec Raynald. There was only one answer remaining—the one for which his relentless second-in-command now stood waiting.

He brought his glance wearily back to his companion. "All right, Jackson," he ordered dully, *"take over."*

It should have been a discomfiting fact to both officers that in view of their previous ugliness, the Cheyenne men now made no trouble over the imprisonment of their women and children. But Jackson assumed it was his two companies of bayonet-issued troopers and his own feared presence which guaranteed the uneasy truce, while Weston took softer comfort from the supposition that the Indians were grateful for the chance to see and talk to their loved ones.

If certain of the squaws were greeted with selective fervor and if several of the cradleboard infants received a more detailed welcome than others, neither the Major nor the Captain made anything of it.

For their parts the braves could not be blamed if they sought to make sure, under the covering emotion of squeezing some particularly buxom squaw or fondling an especially appealing little one, that the latter still had the small trinkets of wood and metal given them on the band's departure from the Clear Fork campsite. If, while a man's right hand was patting a favored mate's buttocks, his left was probing between her breasts to determine if the dismantled frame or polished trigger-spring of a Colt patent revolver still hung pendant there, who could reasonably censure him? And should another brave's searching fingers slide beneath the lacings of a cradleboard while he held his little son close, to make sure that the buttstock or barrel of a Winchester rifle was yet in secret place, what visible harm in that?

Unfortunately for their white jailers, there appeared to be none.

Had Crook been there it might have been a different story. But Three Stars was still in Laramie and he had forgotten to tell Weston one most important thing about Plains Indians: children they might be; fools they were not. And the Cheyenne would have been worse than fools not to welcome the hidden arrival of five perfectly good rifles and eleven serviceable revolvers.

With the last member of the tribe safe in B barracks Jackson ordered the hasp made fast and the work begun on boarding the windows. Only when the latter task was completed and the chain guard in place—a picked trooper stationed every forty feet around the building—did he inform Dull Knife of Weston's unwilling ultimatum: no food and no water until the rebellion was completely controlled by the Indians themselves.

When it was so controlled, and in consideration of a signed paper from the Council of Elders that no further escapes would be attempted and that the tribe would at once and peaceably prepare to return to Oklahoma, their former freedoms and regular rations would be restored. To guarantee the pledge Dull Knife and all nine of his subchiefs would be held hostage until the march was organized and under way. If, meantime, a nervous squaw or warrior should flee the post or otherwise break the terms of the truce, one of the ten hostages would be shot, and one would continue to be shot for every adult Indian not present or accounted for at roll call.

The Cheyenne received the conditions in echoing silence.

They would not even answer Jackson to let him know they understood what he was saying, much less to inform him whether or not they would accept Weston's harsh offer. But finally, in reply to a dramatic plea from Alec Raynald who had married a Cut Arm woman and was, though they might threaten to kill him and mean it literally, trusted by the Cheyenne, Dull Knife came to one of the windows.

The boarding planks were spaced roughly about a foot apart, allowing the Pine Ridge interpreter to see the old man clearly. Raynald make the peace sign toward him, following it with the brow-touch of respect. "I am sorry about all this, my brother," he called to him in Cheyenne. "You and I know it is not our fault. But this is a very bad time for our people. You don't want their blood on the ground again, do you?"

"If this ground is made red," replied the old chief sonorously, "we cannot help it. We gave up our guns and we shook hands with the Soldier Chiefs. They told us we could stay here. Now they say we cannot. It will not be our fault if blood is spilled in this place now."

"What you say is not all true," argued Raynald earnestly. "From the first you have known that you would probably have to go back. Major Weston has told you this all the time. Is my tongue not straight?"

"He said he hoped we could stay. That he would try his best to see that we could. Then he said he was sure we could. And all the time I told him that if we could not, we would die first."

"That is true," admitted the other. "But in between he always warned you that perhaps he would fail. I know this, my brother, for I told you so myself. Several times he has had me tell you. Do I lie now when I say this?"

He did not lie, the old chief knew that. Many claims to the contrary would subsequently be made, both by their white sympathizers and by the Indians themselves. But there is no doubt of the record on this one point. From the onset of their arrival at Fort Robinson, Major Howell Weston repeatedly and conscientiously cautioned the Cheyenne not to get their hopes of remaining in the north, too high. But in the dark hour of present realization even Dull Knife's faithful heart was not strong enough to accept the final word of his white brother.

"I do not say you lie," he granted evasively. "I only say this is a terrible thing that White Hair has done to his friends. For ourselves," his wrinkled hand swept the circle of braves who had come up to stand behind him, "we do not care. We are men and we are warriors. Cold and hunger are common food to us. But," he flung his arms wide with the impassioned plea, "here are women and little ones. Here are five babies yet on their mothers' milk. Here are Shy Deer and Bright Song and Lame Woman, all heavy with young. And here is Red Bird's mother who will bear her third child before another sun. What will the babies drink when their mothers' dugs are dry? How will we wash Red Bird's little brother when he comes among us? Where are White Hair's answers to these things he has done to us?"

Raynald shook his head, touched his brow once more toward the outraged Cheyenne. He took the painful care with his words which came only from long experience in dealing with the literal Indian mind. "The answers are not his, old friend," he soothed, "they are *yours*. It is up to you to calm your people and to make them see that Major Weston does not lie and that he has truly done all he can to help them. You have only to give him your word that there will be no trouble and that your people will go back south in peace. If you are his friend and the friend of your own people, you will have to do that. There is no other way, my brother, you know that."

Dull Knife peered at him through the narrow opening between the window boards. He said nothing. The seconds dragged like hours to the perspiring interpreter. Finally, the old chief nodded softly. "*Naheeneno,* my friend. To know a thing is not to make it God's will."

"What do you mean?" asked the white man uncertainly.

"I know that White Hair's heart is good. I know that he can do no more for us. But Maheo will not let me believe it and I cannot lie to my people any longer."

"All right," said Raynald very carefully. "What is your final answer? What is it you want me to tell Major Weston now?"

Dull Knife did not make him wait this time. His words came with difficulty and with obvious emotion but they came unhesitatingly. "Tell him that I am here on my own ground and I will never go back. Tell him that he may kill me here but he cannot make me go back."

"Is that it? Is that *nohetto?*" delayed the Pine Ridge interpreter. "Be very thoughtful now, old friend. Don't hurry your answer. This is a bad place we stand in."

But Dull Knife raised his right hand at once. He chopped it sharply downward in the Cheyenne sign which meant the talk was over, that he was cutting it off.

"*Hehe naheve*," was all he said. "*Nohetto—*"

The next moment only the boarded-up emptiness of the broken window was looking back at Alec Raynald.

CHAPTER 20

B BARRACKS measured exactly eighteen by thirty-six feet. It had been originally built to house twenty-four troops. There was a double tier of bunks along either wall, room in the narrow aisle between them for a Sibley stove and two dozen footlockers. Into this foul-aired pen were now herded 151 Cheyenne men, women and children.

The stoic captives made the best of a grim situation.

The very old squaws, the smaller children and pregnant women were given the bunks. The others stood or squatted or lay curled in shivering misery upon the remaining, bare floor space. Such primitive sanitation as was possible, they practiced. Where the stove had stood, the floor had been cut away to provide a bottom draft. This opening had been subsequently floored over. Its covering boards were now ripped away and the shallow aperture beneath used as a rude toilet. With fastidious Indian discipline the smallest child was made to relieve himself into it. But before the long hours of the first day crawled past the accumulating stench of their own filth became a reeking, nauseous sickness. By dawn, more than one of the grown men had had to excuse himself and go to the hole and vomit into it.

The cold, for the babies and old ones huddled in the bunks and for the women and children crouched near the center of the packed aisle, was not intolerable. But the men and half-grown boys, hunched along the outer edges of the pack beneath the paneless windows, awoke with hoar frost caking their nostrils and with the thick spittle frozen upon their lips where they had licked them in unconscious, slavering hunger.

At first the pangs of advancing starvation were fed with Dull Knife's repeated assurances that with the women and children involved, Weston would relent. The suffering from thirst, less easily assuaged, began to become acute with noon of the first day. Still, the bewildered Cheyenne could not bring themselves to believe their friend White Hair actually meant to deprive them of water.

With nightfall they began to wonder, and to scrape the mounded snow from the window sills and melt it in their parched mouths. With the second dawn even the snow became precious and the scowling subchiefs ordered it rationed among the nursing mothers and two- and three-year-old children. Still there was no word from Major Weston. The 8th of January crept by, hour after stomach-cramping hour. At last the smallest child ceased its weeping, its tiny body dehydrated of tears, its little mind confused and dulled beyond the will to longer answer aloud the demands of its spasming belly. Then, just at sunset, Captain Jackson appeared outside the front windows.

The white officer was alone and demanded at once to speak with Dull Knife. When the old chief came forward he challenged him with brutal directness. Had his mule-headed people had enough? Were the women hungry? The babies thirsty? Was Dull Knife ready to sign the paper and come out in peace?

Jackson's Cheyenne was not fluent but it was frighteningly intelligible. They all heard the foreign awkwardness of his words, they all understood them, they all waited hopefully for Dull Knife's answer to them.

But the latter did not answer. Instead, he questioned demandingly. Where was Evoxpohess? Why did White Hair not come and talk to them? They would not deal with Captain Jackson, only with Major Weston. Where was he? Why did he stay away? Was he afraid to come and look at what he had done to his friends?

Jackson did not prolong the parley. "You'll talk to me or you'll talk to no one!" he broke angrily into English. "Understand that very clearly. I am carrying out Major Weston's orders. I wouldn't be here otherwise. You know that as well as I do. Now speak up and be damned quick about it."

Dull Knife shook his head. "We will talk only to White Hair," he repeated stubbornly.

"All right," grated Jackson, "I'll say it once more. Major Weston won't talk to you again, nor will I until you send for me. When you're ready to talk, inform the sergeant of the guard. He'll send a soldier for me. But I warn you," he added harshly, "don't bother the sergeant or send for me until you're ready to come out!"

He did not wait for Dull Knife's answer but swung away at once and strode off across the parade ground. The old chief watched him go, his heart settling deep and cold within him like an old, tired millstone into dark, still water. He turned slowly from the window, his leathered face composed, the dry-throated croak of his voice gentle and unafraid. But as he raised them toward his waiting followers and unseen by them in the thickening winter twilight, his gnarled hands were trembling.

"My children," he told them quietly, "we have one friend left. Let us talk to him."

Throughout the endless cold of that third night the Cheyenne patriarch crouched with Little Chief and the sacred bundle of the Medicine Arrows in a far corner of the barracks. Sleepless and alone they sat the night away drawing on the fireless bowl of the Holy Pipe and imploring Maheo to hear his children and to answer them. But Maheo said nothing. His only reply was the whistle of the January wind along the snow-piled ridgepole and the passing, frozen crunch of the chain-guards' patrolling footsteps.

By late afternoon of the following day Dull Knife knew the end was very near. His people had been four days and nights without food or water. The old ones were now too weak to move from their bunks. The nursing mothers were forcing their own cottony spittle into the mouths of their little ones so that their tiny, protruding tongues would not swell and strangle them. The older children lay motionless upon the floor along the edges of the bunks, their bellies distended with the toxic gases of starvation, their black eyes dull with the listless fever of coming death by thirst. The grown men and teen-age boys held loose bullets in their mouths, sucking at the acrid bite of the lead to induce the flow of saliva and keep their ballooning tongues from shutting off their breath. When the old chief saw Tangled Hair relieving himself into his moccasin and drinking his own urine he raised his dimming eyes toward the jack-pine rafters and knew that his god had forgotten him.

And that the soldier chiefs had beaten him.

It was 5 P.M. and almost dark when he went to the window and called out to the sergeant of the guard.

Lundy, who had just relieved Meeker, moved forward through the dusk. In response to the tribal leader's request he touched his brow and answered in Cheyenne. To look at the proud old devil now would break the heart of a granite headmarker. It was the least a man could do to pay him the honor of using his own tongue. "I hear you, father," he said humbly. "I will go at once and take your words to Captain Jackson." Dull Knife returned the brow sign, nodded wearily. "An old man thanks you, my son. Tell him we are ready to send a man out to talk."

This time when he hurried up through the settling gloom Jackson did not come alone. Behind him at a chopping dogtrot came a double file of carbine-swinging troopers. "Company halt!" he shouted, waving the order with a slash of his fringed gauntlet. "Break out. I want that doorway flanked right and left. Lundy!"

"Yes sir."

"Get on that door. I want just one Indian to come out of it, you understand? The minute he *is* out, jump your detail between him and the barracks. You got that?"

"Yes sir! All right, you sloughfoots!" he bawled at the nearby sentries. "You heard the Captain, on the double now!"

As the guards stumbled into place at the door Jackson flashed his gauntlet again. "Ready arms!" he snapped to his own squad. The tense troopers ported their Springfields. They flipped their loading traps open and shut in a clicking ripple of metallic sound all the more ominous for the stillness in which it fell. "Arms ready, Captain," signaled their corporal. Jackson stepped toward the door. "All right in there. Send your man out."

Lundy unhasped the padlock, moved quickly aside.

There was a stir of noise from within. The door scraped open. A single Cheyenne stalked out straight and haughty as a buffalo lance, his fierce pride trying desperately to overcome his physical weakness and to let him walk proud.

Dull Knife had chosen his peace talker with dangerous care. It was Wild Hog, the implacable white hater.

He tottered up to Jackson, halting not a foot from him. His first bitter words revealed that Dull Knife's instructions had been as unfortunate as his selection of Wild Hog to convey them. "I am ready!" he snarled at Jackson. "Take me to White Hair."

The white officer recoiled as though the Indian had spit in his face. He stepped back. "I'll *take you,* my friend," he choked. Then, thickly furious to Lundy who had shadowed the scowling brave from the barracks door, *"Grab the bastard!"*

Lundy was a twenty-year man. A career NCO in the regular army. His soul might be his own but his body belonged to the nearest commissioned officer.

He grabbed.

Quick as he was, Wild Hog was quicker.

He twisted and fought like a wild thing, broke free of the big hillman's grasp, dashed crazily back toward the barracks. A nervous trooper near the door hipped his rifle, fired point-blank. Wild Hog stopped as though he had crashed headlong into an invisible wall, seized his ruptured belly with both hands, went down and into the snow without a sound.

In the shock of it the barracks door stood for a moment forgotten and unguarded. It burst open suddenly and Lone Crow sprang out. He broke through Lundy's guard detail, ran toward the fallen Wild Hog. He got only halfway down Jackson's flanking lines of troopers. Two soldiers, one from each side of the double line, leaped forward. Their viciously swung bayonets speared Lone Crow in mid-stride, pinning him like a gaunt red moth between them. The force of the meeting blades lifted the Cheyenne warrior free of the ground, dropped him bleeding and crying aloud in the agony of his wounds, alongside his stricken companion.

It was too much for Left Hand, Lone Crow's inseparable fellow. The ugly-tempered brave who had come within an angry wolf howl of murdering Amy Lohburg did not see the flashing bayonets of the hated Long Knives. He saw only his old friend badly hurt and helpless upon the ground. His old friend and then one other fateful thing. The still open, still unguarded door of B barracks! Growling like a wounded grizzly, Left Hand charged.

Lundy met him just beyond the doorway. Barring his

115

Springfield with both hands, he drove its barrel into the enraged brave's face just above the bridge of the nose. Left Hand staggered back clawing at the blood in his eyes. Lundy stepped swiftly into him, caved in the side of his skull with the Springfield's steel butt plate. The Indian dropped in his tracks, uncomplaining and empty-eyed as a slaughterhouse beef.

Only a heartbeat had passed since the harsh bark of the white officer's order. Yet history in the hands of willful, angry men is never more than a heartbeat from spilled blood. Captain J. T. Jackson was a willful, angry man. For one dark moment he held history in his hands. And the ground was made red at Fort Robinson, Nebraska.

CHAPTER 21

WESTON WAS in the officers' mess with Surgeon Ralph Cummings and three company lieutenants, Travis Benton, Howard Thomas and Jules Stienberg when the muffled shot put a flat period to Cummings's rambling dissertation on the advances in gangrene surgery since Shiloh and Second Manassas.

"That," announced Benton gratuitously, "was a Springfield."

"Sounded like it came from over by B barracks," added Thomas with equal offhandedness.

"Probably one of the rawtails we got in last week," sniffed the third of Weston's young gentlemen. "You'd think the least they could tell a recruit before letting him out of boot camp is that when he pulls that little piece of metal inside the trigger guard, a gun will go off."

Cummings said nothing, leaving it to Weston to make the first relevant comment. "Where's Captain Jackson?" asked the post C.O.

"On duty," replied Stienberg. "At least I saw him in your office on my way over here."

"Just now, Jules?"

"Yes sir, not five minutes ago."

"Good." Weston's relief was obvious. "Ferris is O.D., isn't he?"

"All day long," smiled the youngster, well pleased with what he felt was, present company considered, a rather neat riposte. Weston was in no mood for anemic bons mots. "Do any of you know who has the guard detail at the barracks?" he frowned.

"Meeker just came off," shrugged Benton. "Damned if I know who went on."

"I think we had better find out," worried Weston out loud. "Soldier—"

The nearest mess orderly hurried up. "Yes sir?"

"Run over to my office, please. Ask Lieutenant Ferris to come over here."

The orderly had only begun his salute when the mess door banged open to admit the officer in question. As Howell Weston's A.G., Frank Ferris ordinarily had his share of troubles. When his turn as officer of the day rolled around, those worries doubled. And when Captain Jackson was acting in command for Major Weston, a man's official difficulties multiplied past computation. Right now the young adjutant's woes were piling up faster than his conscience could sort them out. "Beg pardon, Major," he blurted, "did you hear that shot just now?"

"We heard it, Frank. What's up?"

"It's Captain Jackson, sir."

"*What!*"

"Yes sir. He just went over to B barracks."

Weston came to his feet. "I think we had better get over there *with* him, gentlemen," he tersely instructed his lieutenants. "Let's go."

"Wait a minute, Major," Ferris gestured nervously. "You don't quite understand. Captain Jackson went over there *before* the shot."

Weston blanched, swung around. "Who relieved Meeker on the guard detail?" he asked quietly.

"Lundy, sir. I doubt if there's any real trouble. I just thought you ought to know about the Captain being over there." Then, in belated defense, "Lundy sent for him."

"All the *more* reason," said Weston curtly, "for getting over there ourselves. Gentlemen, please come along." He had not reached the door when it banged open for the second time in as many minutes.

Jackson strode in, eyed Weston's group, directed his calm advice to the still seated Cummings. "Major Cummings, I believe you had better join Major Weston's party. There are three pretty sick Indians over there in front of B barracks."

The post physician got up hurriedly and left, the three lieutenants accompanying him. Weston waited until Ferris had followed them out and closed the door behind him. "All right, Jackson," he said, gray eyes leveling on the latter, "what happened?"

"Nothing much, fortunately. They sent me word they were ready to talk. The Indian who came out got nervous and made a break for it. Taylor shot him in the belly. Two more of them ran out of the barracks. We had to put the steel to one and a rifle butt to the other."

"Good Lord, good Lord," Weston murmured softly to himself.

"Yes," agreed his junior, unperturbed, "it looked like touch and go for a minute. However, seeing their three friends stretched in the snow seemed to take the starch out of the others. At least none of them offered to take up the argument. Right now," he concluded cynically, "it's very peaceful over there."

"I see. How badly hurt are they, Jackson?" It was typical of Robinson's soft-spoken C.O. that he thought first of the injured Cheyenne. The fact his own future had just been bayoneted and shot in the belly was entirely clear to him. Equally clear was the fact that a good commander looks to his own wounds last. Both considerations were lost on Jackson.

"The one with the cracked head," he answered feelinglessly, "is unconscious. Hard to tell about him just yet. The bayoneted one will be all right. He got it in the fleshy part of the buttocks from one side, the leg from the other. I don't know about the first one. He got it in a pretty bad place. However," he concluded, "he was still kicking when I left." Something in the almost cheerful way he said it triggered Howell Weston's rare temper. "You don't appear particularly concerned, Captain," he snapped. "Do you enjoy shooting down unarmed hostages?"

With one of those odd quirks of honesty which were continually surprising his C.O., the blond youth turned serious. "You know better than that, Major. There are over 150 Cheyenne in that barracks. They've been without water for four days and they've repeatedly warned us they'll die before they go back south."

"But good heavens, Jackson—!"

"I'm sorry, sir. There are simply no 'buts' to it. If you have to kill one or two of them to keep from killing all of them, it's a cheap price to pay for your command. At any rate," there was a canny return to his normal ambition in the last of it, "I'll sign the report and take full responsibility."

"Well, Jackson," there was no real hope in it but only a growing weariness, "maybe we're getting ahead of ourselves. Perhaps they'll recover."

"We'll soon know," nodded Jackson.

He had no more than said it than the door scraped open. Cummings put his head in, delivered his professional report and prognosis all in the same disappointed scowl. "Just dropped by to give you the bad news," he grumped. "They'll live."

"Thank God," muttered Weston. "How serious are their wounds, Ralph?"

"Well, the one ought to be dead of shock right now and would be if he were a white man. But the bullet was too high to smash the pelvis, too low to nick the kidneys. I don't think it did a damn thing but pass through him. He's already stopped bleeding. The one Lundy dropped is coming around. The other is already on his feet; walked over to the infirmary by himself. They're brute animals. No more fear or feeling in them than a dumb steer. Some of our boys who saw the hole in the first one's belly are sicker than he is. Good night, damn it!" He slammed the door on the curse, grumbled off toward the infirmary.

Weston looked at Jackson, quietly put the remaining question. "Well, that's that. Where do we go from here, boy?"

"No place," rapped the latter confidently. "If you want my opinion, Major, we're out of the woods. I'll guarantee you not another bloody Cheyenne will stick his nose out of B barracks door."

Weston thought uneasily of some of his junior's previous opinions and guarantees about these same Cheyenne. And forced the thought aside. That was a long time ago. The lad had learned a lot about Indians since then. As of 6 P.M., January 9, 1879, Captain J. T. Jackson ought to know what he was talking about. And a man could gratefully believe that his present promise would hold firm.

Literally speaking, it did.

Not another Cheyenne ever came out of B barracks padlocked door and Captain Jackson's last guarantee was never broken.

But that guarantee covered only doors.

It said nothing about windows.

The wind died with the sun that night. The moon came very early. By its wan light, the Cheyenne made ready.

An hour before, while the blood of Lone Crow and Wild Hog and Left Hand was yet warm upon the snow beyond the barracks door, the Council of Elders had gathered for the last time around Dull Knife. In the time it took Little Chief to make the four sacred signs and consult the pipe, the vote had gone around the slit-eyed circle. When the medicine man announced that without true smoke the pipe was telling him nothing, it remained only for Dull Knife to put the council's decision before the waiting women, children and old ones.

"We must all die now." he told them simply. "But we will not die shut up in this soldier house like dogs. We will die in the open and die fighting."

It was Wild Hog's grieving woman who answered for all his listeners and who said it even more simply than had her chief. *"We will die like Cheyenne,"* amended the gaunt squaw.

Now, while the women saw to the last readying of the children—smiling away their fears, singing them low-voiced brave songs, telling them the favorite happy stories—the men and older boys crouched in the far end of the building at grimmer business.

A squat brave named Shield had just been appointed War Chief. Shield, like the wounded Lone Crow, had been a scout for Crook against the Sioux in '76 and '77. He knew his way around the immediate confines of Fort Robinson as well as a sightless squaw knew the inside of her own lodge. Beyond the fort, he could call the exact distance and direction of every prairie signpost within a month's march. He was a fierce and determined fighter, afraid of no Indian, fearing no Pony Soldier. Every warrior listened carefully as he told them how it was going to be.

"Behind this place," he pointed toward the rear wall of the barracks, "lies open snowland and then the river." He referred to the upper channel of the White which ran just west of the post. "When we have crossed the stream we will all come to-

120

gether and make for the bluffs on the other side. But on this side of the water the soldiers have that building where they cut up the trees. Down there they also have a bridge crossing the river. Do you all know it?"

The front row braves nodded and he went on. "We will make our first run for that bridge. Some of the water is running pretty strong and I think the ice may be a little thin and bad out there in the middle. We must see that the women and young ones go by the bridge. Now that will take a little time." Again the swift nods, the terse resumption. "We have five rifles. *Who will shoot them?*"

This time the nods were not so quick. Every brave knew what Shield meant. The five men who shot the rifles would stay behind to block the narrow logging track leading down to the sawmill bridge, buying the necessary time for the women and children to get across. The price they would pay for that time would be their lives.

The hesitation had a hard Indian reason far divorced from any fear of dying. To lose one's life that a comrade might live, to go down fighting while one's women and children made good their escapes, these were the highest Cheyenne privileges. But such honors were not for the aged, the unsteady of hand, the unsure of heart and eye. The five rifles were more precious than fifty warriors. Who got them was a matter of life for a hundred and fifty, not death for five.

As Shield spoke, Little Chief stepped into the center of the circle and laid the reassembled guns upon the floor. The middle rifle was the one Little Wolf had given Red Bird, and the main frame and buttstock of which the boy's mother had smuggled into the barracks under the swollen blanket of her pregnancy. Shield now reached for the War Chief's Winchester, his words as simple as the gesture was selfless. "Naturally, I will take the first one."

Hunts Alone, a morose, unpopular man, picked up the second rifle. "Wild Hog was kind to me one time," he recalled. "I think he was my friend."

"I am a bachelor, I have no one," said Noisy Walking and took up the third gun.

"Well, I have a woman," admitted Big Beaver reluctantly, "but she talks too much. I would rather have a good gun."

When the slow-witted brave had made his brow-knit selection of the remaining rifles Yellow Hawk sneered disdainfully, "You have left the best one, emptyhead," and scooped

121

up the fifth weapon. As if in apologetic defense of his action he shrugged deprecatingly to Dull Knife. "It is just that Hokom-xaaxceta would want me to do it, father. He was always so proud of my eyes."

There was no more talk after that.

The eleven revolvers were passed out silently to the other best shots. Each of the braves opened his warbag and began to paint his face, first putting on the gaudy pigments of his own good-medicine colors and finally the charcoal darkness of the *emeoestove*—the death color, the black paint.

While the warriors painted their faces the women piled all the equipment that was to be left behind beneath the two front windows. At the last moment each of the men tied two blankets to his body, one around the neck, one around the waist, leaving both hands free to fight. When all were ready Shield gave the signal. His four riflemen divided themselves between the windows, two to the left, two to the right. "Are you ready here?" he whispered to the pair on the left. "The moon is good," grunted Hunts Alone. "I can see the guards clearly." "He speaks for me," nodded Noisy Walking. "A blind man could hit a weanling chipmunk in this light."

"And here?" rasped Shield, joining the others at the right window. "Can you see them well from here?"

"Mine is already dead," said Yellow Hawk, his famous eyes narrowed along his rifle barrel following the tread of the nearest sentry. "Well, now, cousin," admitted Big Beaver graciously, "you are a little ahead of me. Mine is still alive. But then you have the best rifle," he qualified soberly. "However, I think this one I am watching will not feel very good presently. I think his woman will be weeping before long. I remember one time we were up on the Musselshell River stealing horses from the Crows. It was just such a fine moonlight as this one. I shot five of the enemy that night. Of course one was a squaw but I did not know that until later. You see I thought she was—"

"Shut up, you fool!" hissed Shield. "I did not ask you how to steal a horse!"

"He lies anyway," said Yellow Hawk, not taking his eyes from his rifle barrel. "I was on that trip. He only shot three and *two* of them were squaws."

"*Aii-eee,*" sighed Big Beaver resignedly, "I am ready, brother."

122

Shield turned his head, signaled quickly to Dull Knife. "All right, father, we are ready now."

The old chief stepped into a little patch of moonlight slanting along the center aisle from the boarded windows. "Pray with me," he told his waiting people. "We are going now and it is time to say goodbye."

Outside the barracks, two of the patrolling sentries came to a startled halt as their paths met and as the eerie chant of the Cheyenne Death Song stole across the sudden stillness.

"*Jazus Murphy!*" gasped the first soldier, his brogue held unconsciously low, the short hairs along the nape of his neck rising instinctively. "What in the name of hivvin are they doin' in there? Holdin' a red Injun wake or somethin'?"

The second trooper had been with Crook and Mackenzie when the latter had trapped and burned Dull Knife's village on the Red Fork of the Powder River in '76. During the black dawn following that shameful slaughter he had heard the prayer of the death song coming from the hillside rocks where the suicide rear guard of the Cheyenne had holed up to delay the pony soldier pursuit. He was furthermore a young man with a good memory, and he was not shivering now because the mercury stood at fourteen degrees below zero. "No, by God," he whispered hoarsely to his companion, "*they're praying!*"

"Faith now," muttered the Irishman crossing himself three times, "they must be jabberin' to the Divil himself. Sure and no Christian God would be listenin' to sich haythen noise!"

Private P. J. O'Shea was right. His Christian God was not listening. That last minute in the moonlight outside B barracks belonged to Maheo.

And to Yellow Hawk.

The Cheyenne brave's rifle spat a vicious amen to the last deep vowel of Dull Knife's prayer. The heavy slug shattered O'Shea's cheekbone, blew the back of his head and his brains out. His companion made a little more noise dying because Big Beaver was not a good enough shot to risk a head-sighting and had to hold low for the broad area of the groin.

In the first seconds six troopers, every man stationed in front of B barracks, were dead or down, and the Cheyenne were pouring through the falling glass and splintering boards of the barracks windows in a hysterically weeping, thirst-maddened rush for the sawmill bridge and the frozen river.

CHAPTER 22

SHIELD DIED first—in a face-close burst of rifle fire from the guards in the rear of the barracks. Running in the pack behind him, Red Bird saw him go down, saw Little Wolf's precious Winchester go spinning from his slack hands. He dove for the gun, swept it up out of the snow, fired from the ground at the soldier towering above him. The man fell across him and a second trooper, lunging at the Cheyenne boy with his bayonet, accidentally drove the steel into his own companion's back. Before he could wrench the blade free, Red Bird shot him through the body.

Big Beaver and Yellow Hawk were leaping over the boy then, killing two of the remaining three guards critically wounding the third and winging the cursing Lundy who had just come racing up from the front of the barracks. Red Bird rolled to his feet in time to see his mother fall heavily, as she ran for the bridge. He stumbled to her side, helped her up, stayed with her until he lost her in the crushing jam on the sawmill span.

Lundy was not dangerously hit but the force of the .44-caliber ball ripping his shoulder spun him off his feet, knocked him headfirst into a shallow snowdrift. He came to his knees spitting frozen dirt, front teeth and boiling Cherokee blood. "All right, you Cheyenne sons of bitches!" he roared, "you just shot the wrong sergeant!"

As officer of the guard, he was wearing one of the late issue Single Action Army Colts. He had never fired the new gun, being a rifleman by hill country preference and service tradition, but under some circumstances—like a damn mad first sergeant seeing the two bucks who had downed him still running for the sawmill bridge—it promised certain advantages over the old reliable Springfield.

Lundy came to his feet clawing for the Colt and leaping toward the bridge. Behind him he heard the shouts of the first troops arriving at B barracks from across the parade ground.

"This way, boys!" he bellowed. "Follow me! Hit for the saw-mill bridge!"

He recognized Meeker's ringing yell and his answering "Give 'em hell, Cherokee, we're right behind you!" then he was diving off the logging track into a clump of cottonwoods, with the lead of the Cheyenne rear guard at the bridgehead cutting the snow from under his racing feet. The next minute Meeker and half a dozen G Troop regulars were tumbling in beside him.

"That bunch yonder is trying to hold the bridge," he barked at his fellow sergeant, "four, maybe five of them. They're all picked hardtails and they've all got repeating rifles." He gathered his long legs under him. "One of the scuts drilled me," he added quietly. "I aim to see if he'd like to try for another seegar. Let's go." With the grunted order, he went up and out of the cottonwood gully, Meeker and two of the troopers piling after him.

Where they broke into the open moonlight of the logging track, they were less than thirty feet from the Cheyenne death squad. Yellow Hawk got both of the troopers before Lundy's Colt blew his face away at arm's length. Meeker shot Hunts Alone through both lungs, bayoneted Big Beaver off the side of the bridge-ramp. The good-natured brave fell onto the ragged shore ice and Meeker, scooping off one of the fallen soldier's Springfields, shot him in the head as he staggered back to his feet.

Noisy Walking, the last of the suicide warriors, threw his empty Winchester at Lundy, flashed his hidden scalping knife and came for him. He was too close. The giant Oklahoman could not sidestep him. He swung his hip into him, taking the blade in the muscle of the buttock. Twisting around, he circled the lunging brave's throat with his left arm, flung him around, jammed the Colt into the small of his back and shot him twice through the spine.

He threw the lifeless body from him, whirled in time to hear Meeker calling him from the edge of the ramp. "Down here, Johnny! We've got a crawler!" He stepped over to the other sergeant and Meeker growled, "Here, gimme that pop-gun."

Glancing below the ramp, Lundy saw Hunts Alone crawling on the river ice, where he had jumped from the bridge. The Cheyenne was whimpering like a hurt animal, dragging himself blindly around in a circle, coughing and strangling

125

on the blood welling from his crushed lungs. Lundy gritted his teeth, handed the Colt to Meeker. The little noncom steadied both hands on the bridge rail, put the three remaining shots into the stricken Indian. "Shoots a shade left of center," he observed, handing the gun back. "Let's get the hell out of here."

"Correct on both counts," muttered Lundy. "You see what I see, coming yonder?" As his companion hesitated, peering across the bridge, Lundy grabbed him. "Get down!" he rasped, pulling him below the rise of the ramp. *"Now* look— and be damn short about it!"

Meeker raised his head, took a brief look along the length of the span toward the far side. He ducked back, losing color even in the moonlight. "Jeez! here they come!" he hissed. "They must be after them rifles the others dropped."

"They can have 'em," was Lundy's brief opinion. "No use being a hawg about it." He rolled over the edge of the ramp to the snow of the riverbank below, Meeker following him, both of them burrowing in under the timbers of the ramp. They made themselves very small and very quiet and got along on what air they had in their lungs at the moment of the retreat.

Overhead, a party of ten Cheyenne, headed by Tangled Hair, raced to a halt. There was half a minute of guttural conversation and furious searching for the priceless rifles of their dead comrades. Then, with all four of the guns recovered, the last one from alongside Big Beaver's body not ten feet from the breath-held sergeants, the Cheyenne were gone as swiftly as they had returned.

"My sentiments precisely, Johnny," exhaled Meeker, in delayed reply to Lundy's interrupted opinion on reclaimed rifles. "Why be a pig about a lousy handful of secondhand Winchesters? Or a short-dozen wild-hair hostiles, for that matter? They'll still be plenty of Injuns to go around by the time General John Tenney Custer gets his boys mounted up and under way, back yonder. Meantime," he added thoughtfully, "I reckon I'll just wait up for the dear Captain, right here."

"That shines, Sam," agreed his brother noncom, as considerately. "I allow me and you has had our feet in the trough just about long enough for one night. Besides," his voice was suddenly hard, "I ain't got no belly for what's coming to them poor devils down there, now." He nodded toward the river and its fringing timber, finished softly. "You got the makings, pardner?"

"A little for my own personal use."

"Thanks. You always was a sentimental slob."

The two old soldiers got out their pipes, loaded them from Meeker's pouch, smoked in short, deep drags, holding the smoke in their lungs a long time, carefully breaking it up with their hands when they let it out. And all the while they watched and listened to what Sergeant Lundy had no belly for.

Up and down the stream from the bridge, the cries and struggles of the crossing Cheyenne could still be heard and seen. Perhaps half of them, including most of the younger women and older children, had escaped safely across the bridge ahead of Lundy's and Meeker's arrival. But the rest of the band, in particular the old men and squaws and the smaller children lost from their parents in the darkness, had missed the bridge and had to blunder across the stream where they struck it.

Many broke through the treacherous ice. Some drowned, a few got on across. The weaker and less resolute of the elders and nearly all of the children with them, tortured by uncontrollable thirst, threw themselves at the edge of the nearest ice break and drank their shrunken bellies full of the swirling black water.

These stragglers paid a swift and terrible price for their first drink in four days.

While Lundy and Meeker crouched beneath the ramp of the sawmill bridge listening to their desperate splashings, the first of the running troops from the main barracks tumbled down the logging road toward the deserted span. Some crossed on over, to fan out in the timber along the far side. The others deployed along the near bank, north and south from the bridgehead. Their beginning rifle fire was thin and spotty. Soon it picked up. For a long ten minutes it barked and snarled along the White at a rate approaching timed company fire. Then it fell away into absolute stillness.

The hidden sergeants listened a full minute after the last shot. The only sounds to break the eerie silence were white sounds—the voices of the company commanders calling and countercalling the identifications of their outfits in the blackness of the timber above and below the bridge. In all the other long-drawn quiet, there was no Indian sound. No frightened splashing in midstream, no crack of giving ice or old one's despairing cry, no lost, high voice of terrified child.

They knocked the burnt dottle out of their pipes, picked up

their rifles, crawled back out onto the empty moonlight of the bridge.

Neither of them said anything, or needed to. Both had been here before. Each knew what that stillness spelled. The only Cheyenne still within Springfield range of the White River were safely beyond any dread of thirst or hunger, long past all fear of Fort Robinson's avenging pony soldiers.

Within fifteen minutes, Jackson had his pursuit column double-timing over the sawmill bridge. He and Weston headed the troops. In front of them were Alec Raynald and his three Sioux trackers from Pine Ridge. Four inches of fresh snow lay on the ground. The wind was dead still. The thermometer hovered at fifteen below. In the daybright glare of the winter moon, the Cheyenne sign read mercilessly clear.

Beyond the bridge, heading for the low bluffs to the west, the warriors had begun to whip the Cheyenne survivors together and to get them traveling in a roughly formed column. With this heavier sign aiding them, the Sioux trackers picked up speed and, as the bluffs loomed ahead, Jackson panted to his stumbling superior, "If I know them, Weston, they will be holed up in those bluffs. That's why I wanted to push them on foot. Had we waited to mount a column, they would have been halfway to Wyoming before we got off the post. This way, we'll be back in the barracks within an hour—*and so will they!* You'll see, by God," he trailed off grimly.

Weston said nothing. He was not an Indian fighter. He knew nothing, actually, about the Cheyenne except that they preferred their meat boiled, took a little coffee with their sugar, were kind to their children and made beautiful bearskin coats. He had covertly turned over the command to Jackson on his return from Laramie, knew, helplessly, that this was no time to reconsider the decision. Rather, and far rather, it was a time to listen to his tough-minded junior and to learn a little something about handling rebellious hostiles.

Which is what he did learn in the following thirty minutes —and quite a little something.

When it was all over, a man had to admit that Jackson had been partly right. The troops *were* back in their barracks and not an hour had passed. But they were back without any *live* Cheyenne. And with the stiffening bodies of their own dead, plus an additional half-dozen wounded, jolting in the bed of a hurriedly brought up field ambulance.

At the bluffs, the Cheyenne had stopped the white column in its tracks. They had given the troops nothing to fire at save the muzzle flashes of their guns—and these never twice in the same place or split second. It had been like fighting ghosts, and the Robinson command, made up largely of new replacements from Fort Lincoln, had exhibited very little stomach for trading shots with the other world.

When, within the first half hour, they had taken their eighth casualty without once having come within howitzer range of zeroing-in on a solitary Indian, even Jackson knew it was the wrong time of night to be proving a Cheyenne point. True to form, he put on a good show of being upset when Weston suggested they break off the action. But, being generally a good soldier and always a smart one, he relayed the order to his lieutenants with exemplary obedience, and with, of course, gracious care to see that Major Weston got full credit for the following retreat.

The only member of the Fort Robinson staff well pleased with the entire affair was Surgeon Ralph Cummings. Three of the severely wounded soldiers presented unusual challenges to his surgical reputation. The kerosene operating lamps in the infirmary burned until 3 A.M., and though he blundered on one of the troopers, raising the command's K.I.A. report to ten, he got the other two safely out of shock and into the hospital cots well before daybreak. As for the boy who died on the table, who would ever question the slip of the experimenting knife which killed him? Or demand to have his bloodless body posted?

Like Jackson, Cummings could bury his mistakes. And did. Along with his three comrades who had fallen at the bluffs the night before, the dead boy was pried into the icy ground of the post cemetery the next dawn—even as Captain J. T. Jackson and Major Howell Weston headed their long column of blue-clad cavalry, foot-slogging infantry and mule-drawn artillery across the sawmill bridge and westward, around the White River bluffs, toward the distant Powder.

CHAPTER 23

THE TRAIL was well marked. It did not take a Sioux tracker to read it. Or an experienced Indian fighter to follow it. Even Howell Weston could see that bloodstained path of despair.

As if the reddened snow were not enough, the black spoor of death itself lay along every mile. But four o'clock the afternoon of the 10th, the troop column was sixteen miles due west of Fort Robinson and Weston, consulting his watch at its head, had counted the huddled bodies of fifteen Cheyenne since leaving the White at daybreak. The majority of these, upon examination, proved to be unwounded. They had simply dropped out of the Indian line of march and frozen to death where they fell.

For Lundy, riding with Weston, the snowdrifted bodies marked more than the miles of the Cheyenne flight. They warned of its desperation. A plains Indian would never leave his dead upon the field unless it meant his own life to do otherwise. The fact that the Cheyenne had made no effort to carry their fallen, or even to cover them, told Lundy the sinister time of day far more accurately than could Weston's pocket watch. Squinting into the sun, he heeled his horse closer to the column commander's. "Best hold up here a minute, Major," he muttered.

The latter did not argue. Waving the halt back to the following troops, he pulled his horse in. "What's the matter?" he asked.

Lundy pointed ahead. "You see that low rise up yonder? The one with them limestone outcrops and scrub timber atop it? Put your glasses on it and tell me what you see."

Weston unslung his field glasses, steadied them on the rocky height. "Nothing," he said shortly. "Why?"

"Take another look."

He refocused the glasses. "There's not a blessed thing on that hill except the tracks of the Indians going up and across it."

"Them glasses ain't that good, Major. They cain't see *across* that rise, just *up* it."

"Say what you mean, man!" demanded Weston irritably. "The troops will be getting restless."

"There ain't no Cheyenne tracks coming down the far side of that hill," said Lundy flatly.

Weston got the point. "You think they're waiting for us up there?"

"No sir. I know they are."

"I can't believe it. That hill is in wide open country. There's not a stick of cover within half a mile of it."

"Not for us there ain't," said his companion quietly.

The Robinson C.O. was with a good teacher and he was learning fast. "I see," he murmured nervously. "What do we do now?"

"Follow on in until we're just out of rifle range. Then scout the far side of the rise for tracks. If the snow's clean over there, we set up the howitzers on this side and start dusting off them topside boulders. We got an hour of daylight yet."

"All right, relay that back to Jackson. I'll ride ahead meantime."

"It'll be a short relay," grinned Lundy. "Yonder comes Yellow Hair now."

The caustic reference was to Jackson and his unwitting emulation of the original "Yellow Hair." But Weston was as ignorant of the Sioux's colorful name for Custer as he was innocent of Jackson's mimicry of the famous head of the Seventh. He made nothing of Lundy's sneer as he braced himself for the scowling Captain's arrival.

"*Now* what the hell is holding us up?" the latter greeted Weston with typical respect. "I thought you were supposed to be a tracker, Lundy!" He wheeled on the big sergeant. "Can't Raynald and his damn Indians drop back for a rest without you losing the line? My God, it's right there in front of you. A blind man could see it."

"That's right, Captain. Only I ain't blind."

"Watch yourself, soldier! You're talking to *me!*" He said it looking at Lundy. But he meant it for Weston. If the latter understood the biting distinction, he did not challenge it. "Lundy thinks the Cheyenne are dug in on top of that hill up ahead," he told the younger officer quietly. "I agree. We will go on up and give it a pounding with the howitzers while we still have light."

"Now wait a minute," grated Jackson. "I've been looking at that hill too. Their trail appears to go right on up and over it. If it does and we fool around getting the artillery set up now we will lose our chance to catch them in the open on the other side. Raynald tells me we're not an hour behind them. That means they can't be far beyond the hill. You can see there's no decent cover for two miles west of it."

"That's right, sir," agreed Lundy with unwonted deference.

"Of course it's right. Any fool can see that. Now I suggest we—"

"Only," continued the tall sergeant calmly, "I ain't no fool. And them Injuns ain't in no open on no far side of no hill."

"You insolent bastard!" flared Jackson. "When I want your advice I'll ask for it. Do you understand that, goddam you! Now then, Weston, I say that we—"

This time it was not Lundy who broke him off. It was Weston and he made it official. "Captain Jackson, you will not curse the men, and you will relay my instructions back to the column. That is an order, sir."

Jackson flushed, fought for control, barely managed to achieve it. "Yes sir," he glared. Then, wheeling his horse on Lundy. "I beg your pardon, Colonel Lundy, sir." He saluted the unhappy noncom. "I promise it won't happen again, sir." With the sardonic gesture and the bitter sneer which backed it, he drove his horse between them, galloped him toward the stalled column.

Watching him go, Weston shook his head. "He's far and away a better soldier than I, Lundy. I only wish he weren't so hard-headed." They turned their horses and rode forward in silence for several seconds before Lundy answered. "It ain't his head that's hard, Major," he said at last.

"Eh?" queried Weston.

"It's his heart, providing he's got one. And that ain't all."

"Yes?"

The big sergeant let another pause jog by, his homely face thoughtful. When he spoke, it was not the words but the soft way he said them that Weston remembered.

"He ain't half the soldier you are, Major."

There were no Cheyenne tracks in the snow beyond the hill. The howitzers were brought up. For forty-five minutes and until darkness blotted out the target, they pounded the top of the elevation. There was not a sound or a sight of Indian movement in response to the shelling. Upward of a hundred rounds of six-pound grapeshot were dumped onto the hilltop before the light went and Weston ordered the battery silenced.

It did not seem possible that a living thing could have survived the murderous way Captain Martin Hayes walked that creeping barrage up and over the hill and back across it, yard by rock-bursting yard. Yet, when the throats of his howitzers were swabbed out and Meeker led a volunteer patrol up the shell-pocked face of the rise, five Cheyenne rifles stabbed instantly downward.

Meeker's squad piled off their horses, hit the dirt and froze, their trained cavalry mounts standing motionless above them. "I'll personally kill the first mother's son of you that fires back!" snarled the little sergeant. "Who got hit?"

"Brown, Sarge," whispered one of the troopers, edging up through the darkness. "They drilled his horse, too. The horse is down up yonder. Clete's pinned under him mortal hard."

"I don't give a damn how hard he's pinned, you idiot. How bad's he hit?"

"Don't know. Clete, he wasn't saying nothing."

"The horse dead?"

"He wasn't thrashing around none."

"All right, don't worry. We'll get Clete loose. Let's go. Over this way. There's a ravine here that we can follow up."

He slid into the gully, the troopers bellying after him. Five yards up the slope, they found the dead mount and his trapped rider. When they got Clete free, they were glad it was too dark to see. It was bad enough to *feel* that leg that had been under the horse. Meeker winced, passed his hand deftly over the rest of the boy's body. Twice more, it came away wet and warm. "One in the chest, one in the face," he said. "He won't know we done it for him, but we'll lug him in with us. Those red buzzards will be down here directly, to cut up the horse," he explained grimly. "We dassn't leave Clete."

They dragged the dying boy down the ravine, got him across Meeker's horse. "Mount up and get the hell shut of here," he told them hoarsely. "See you make a little fuss getting out, so's they'll tail you with their fire. It'll give me and Clete a mite better shake. I'm going to walk him in by hand, so's not to jar him."

Swinging up, the troopers dug out on the gallop. The Cheyenne rifles picked them up at once but scored no more hits. Under cover of the firing, Meeker managed to get the loaded horse down the rise and safely back to the white lines. It was close, quick work. But not close nor quick enough for trooper Cletus Brown. The boy was dead when Surgeon Cummings wiped his exploring hands, stepped back and growled, "He was lucky."

"*Lucky!*" raged Meeker, confronting him whitefaced.

"The leg would have done the job by itself," said Cummings gruffly, "and taken a week longer to do it. Come back and see me after a bit, Meeker. I'll give you something for those nerves."

"Sorry, Doc," muttered the balding noncom. "I reckon they got me snapping where I ain't bit. He was a hell of a nice kid."

"We're all sorry," said Weston gently. "Forget it, Meeker. Lundy—"

"Yes sir."

"How many casualties does that make?"

"Eleven for sure. With ten still in the infirmary."

"Six critical, three serious, one slight," qualified Cummings.

"It's eleven too many," said Weston slowly. "We won't take any more chances."

Lundy shadowed him off through the darkness. "Wait up a minute, Major," he called. Then, coming up to him and dropping his voice. "What do you mean we won't take any more chances?"

"Just that, Lundy. From here on, we'll trail them until they surrender. We'll keep them under pressure with the howitzers but we won't attack. They can't get away and I'll not take another casualty simply to save time."

Reaching impulsively, Lundy found his arm.

"Lookit here, Major, it ain't *time* you need to save." He paused to let it sink in, went on quickly. "We ain't none of us asking for no favors and you ain't going to live long enough to *trail* them Injuns into giving up. When they leave their dead behind like they been doing, they're meaning to die themselves. It's the way they think." Again the pause, and the even quicker resumption. "You're going to have to go on in and clean them out to the last growed buck, shirttail kid and dry-tit squaw among 'em. Damn it all, there simply ain't no other way on God's green prairie for you to hang on to what's left of your command, Hollie!"

The old war-days name slipped out unconsciously. He had not used it since Weston's arrival at Sidney Barracks and, embarrassed now by the awkward silence which followed its unfamiliar sound, he stepped back and dropped his hand away from the latter's arm.

In turn, Weston gripped him by the shoulder.

"Thanks, John, but it's already too late for that. I don't have a command any more."

"You don't *what?*" snorted Lundy in honest surprise, and as though thinking the other was joking.

"I don't have a command any more," repeated Weston dully. "I gave it to Captain Jackson four days ago."

With the cryptic statement, he turned away and was gone. Lundy said nothing, just stood and stared after him, his slow mind turning on but one dead-sure certainty.

If it *was* a joke the Fort Robinson C.O. intended, he had picked a very unfunny time to pull it.

Sometime during the hour of darkness between sunset and moonrise, the Cheyenne came down the slope and cut up the dead horse. And sometime between the latter hour and dawn of the 11th, refreshed by the frozen blood and raw flesh of their first food since Jackson's starvation order, they got off of "Howitzer Hill" and escaped again to the west.

All that Weston's startled staff found among the shattered rocks upon the hilltop were a dozen shell craters and the torn parts of five Cheyenne bodies. Of the butchered horse, there was no hair or shred of hide remaining. The Indians had carried away every bone, tendon and hoof-scrap of the slaughtered animal, including the paunch and entrails with their partly digested contents.

The only thing of professional interest found on the hill was a sixth Cheyenne body; and this, a matter of medical, not military curiosity.

"Hmmm," said Surgeon Cummings, using the toe of his boot to turn the body of the day-old infant. "Born yesterday, froze to death last night, and his mother still on her feet and running. God! The vitality of those women."

"Maybe it was born dead," suggested his orderly hopefully. "Poor little thing—"

"Perfectly normal birth," grumped Cummings. "The umbilicus had already started to close and clot. Would have been open in a still-bearing. No, it lived ten or twelve hours. Hmmm, too damn bad. Well, Jacobs, let's get out of here."

The orderly hung back, staring down at the tiny form.

Glancing guiltily around, to make sure no one saw him, he gently lifted the dead infant, lowered it into a nearby shell crater, mercifully covered it over with the new-fallen snow. When he had finished, he went away quickly and without looking back. It was all the grave ever given Red Bird's little brother.

One other brief event took place before the command left the hill.

It was a little thing and never made the history books. But in similar small moments of command decision, half the Indian history of the frontier has been written. If Custer had waited for Terry . . . if Crazy Horse had charged once more on the Rosebud . . . if the ridgepole of Hanrahan's Saloon had not cracked the night before Adobe Walls . . . if Fetterman had stayed inside Fort Kearney . . . if Black Kettle had not trusted Chivington at Sand Springs. But there is no end to the "ifs" in the Indian tragedy.

Weston and Jackson stood on the western rim of Howitzer Hill, studying the long line of Cheyenne tracks stretching away toward the Powder. The latter was the first to lower his glasses. "Well," he challenged, "now what?"

"I'm going after them, of course." Weston, still scanning the distant trail, said it so casually his companion missed the use of the singular pronoun.

"Good!" he said sharply. "I'll go down and get the column moving."

Weston took down his glasses. "I said *I* was going after them, Captain."

"You what?" demanded Jackson incredulously.

"I am going after the Cheyenne. *You* are going back to Fort Robinson."

Jackson's reaction was immediate and profanely insubordinate. Weston waited him out, repeated the quiet order. With some even quieter additions.

Captain J. T. Jackson was going back to the post. Major Howell Weston was heading west after the Cheyenne. He would take G and H troops of the cavalry (Lundy's and Meeker's) plus Captain Hayes's mounted artillery company. Lieutenants Stienberg and Merle Davis would follow him with C and D Rifle Companies of the Fourteenth Infantry, in dismounted reserve. Jackson would take the remaining cavalry, F and G Troops of the Third, return at once to Robinson, secure the post and begin the mopping up operations there.

When Weston got back, they would add up their respective scores, see definitely where the command stood, turn in the end total to Crook at Laramie. Until that time and lacking that total, they had best not bother the General.

Jackson cursed, threatened, wheedled, even resorted to hard, honest combat logic. Save for where its angry expulsion turned to frost vapor in the freezing cold of the morning air, he wasted his breath. In the end he turned away without a word, swung up on his horse, put him to plunging headlong down the hillside.

Lundy, coming up for orders in time to get a good look at the color of the Captain's handsome face and the shank-deep way he jammed his spurs into his startled horse, grinned happily. "Nothing he won't choke on, I hope," he nodded to Weston.

"If he does," replied the latter pleasantly, "you can take credit for it, sir."

The sergeant's small eyes narrowed. Something had happened to the C.O. since they had parted the evening before. Lundy had not heard him talk that easy, old-time way, or look so smilingly sure of himself, since he had stepped down on the depot platform at Sidney Barracks.

"How come, Major?" he asked wonderingly.

"You remember our talk last night? It put me to thinking, John——" His face clouded, smoothed quickly. "Well, no use going into all that. A man can't live it over. Anyway," the shy, twisting smile his listener had not seen for weeks crooked his mouth corners, "I've just done something I should have done four months ago."

"Sir?" said Lundy, still not up with the pace.

"Taken command," said Howell Weston, and reached for his horse's trailing reins.

CHAPTER 24

WESTON DETAILED Alec Raynald and his Sioux scouts to Jackson's command. While it was a certainty that Dull Knife

137

and the main force composed the band on Howitzer Hill, it was suspected that many of the older Cheyenne, together with some of the smaller children, had become separated from the Indian column during the first night's march west of the White and were still at large somewhere to the rear. In the relentless drive to put and keep pressure on the old chief's group during those first hours, there had been no time to throw out flankers or detach patrols to pick up these stragglers. It now became Jackson's responsibility to do so, using the sober Scot and his three Oglala bloodhounds to trail out the Cheyenne strays while Weston ran the main pack to earth with Lundy's help.

The half-blood Cherokee was well up to the assignment.

For the next five days he kept Weston's troops exactly where the Robinson C.O. wanted them—within close-up, field-glass view, but just beyond effective rifle range of the fleeing Cheyenne.

The Indians made three more stands but the Pony Soldier chief would not come in to them, each time holding his troops back and refusing to risk further casualties. There were a few desultory exchanges of looping, ineffectual rifle fire when his contact patrols crowded the lagging fugitives too closely, and twice more it was necessary to wheel up the howitzers to dislodge the Indians from particularly difficult terrain. Still, Weston kept his word. In the nearly week-long, running fight not another trooper was so much as scratched.

The same could not be said of their desperate quarry.

The white command, examining the last delaying point, following the second use of the howitzers, were convinced that most of the surviving Cheyenne were suffering major shell-burst wounds. In Lundy's bitterly growled hill-country vernacular, the churned up mud and snow of the abandoned Indian position "looked and smelt like the bottom of a settlement pigsty the day after the fall hawg slaughter." Yet not a solitary body marked the trampled site, and the weary troopers knew that dawn would bring only another day of the endless chase.

They were right.

But it was a very short day.

Repeating their previous pattern—holing up at night, slipping through the white lines in the darkness preceding the following daylight—the Cheyenne, that sixth dawn, fled once more westward. Then, with full sunup and the first sight of the inexorable Pony Soldier column closing on them from the east, Dull Knife called the final halt. Atop the rocky, treeless crown of the Hat Creek bluffs, only forty-four miles from the frozen channel of their beloved Powder River, the Cheyenne dug their last rifle pits and prepared to meet both Major Weston and Maheo.

The former did not keep them waiting.

By 7 A.M. his howitzers were pounding the Wyoming blufftops.

Four hours later, Captain Martin Hayes wheeled his artillery out of position and reported back to Weston: from here on it was up to the rifle squads; C Battery, Company F, Fourth Field Artillery, had just lobbed its last shell onto the Hat Creek highlands.

At once Weston ordered Lundy forward with the white flag.

Wiser to the ways of his mother's people than his compassionate commander, the big sergeant kept his horse moving funeral-slow, his small eyes flicking snake-fast.

The sun was at his back, just tipping the blufftops ahead. He saw the warning flash of its rays along the first of the Cheyenne rifle barrels in time to flatten himself behind his mount's neck. The .44-caliber slug whined over him, ricocheted away across the boulder-strewn flats. In the instant it took the Winchester's black-powder report to catch up with its whining lead, he had spun the ungainly bay around and had him in a stretching gallop for the rear.

Forced to the end choice, Weston did not hesitate. It was by now as clear to him as to Dull Knife that Hat Creek marked the last mile north in the long homeward march of the Powder River Cheyenne. As Lundy had warned, they were not going to surrender. As Dull Knife had said, they were never going back to Oklahoma. And as Wild Hog's woman had foretold, they were going to die like Cheyenne.

Weston set his jaw, motioned Lundy forward.

"All right, Sergeant," was all he said, "move in."

Under Lundy and Meeker, G and H Troops of the Third Cavalry invested the bluffs north and south of the Cheyenne position. Lieutenants Benton and Thomas, nominal heads of G and H, went along for the exercise. As in the paying off of most such tactical situations, no less then than now, the sergeants handled the dirty combat cash, the officers took the clean military credit.

The flanking heights commanded the Indian rifle pits by fif-

139

teen feet of elevation. For six straight hours and until the five o'clock dusk cooled their leaded barrels, Weston's eighty Springfield Carbines poured it in. The Cheyenne replied sporadically but their Winchesters were outranged by the harder shooting service arms and their hand-loaded supplies of ammunition were down to the last precious rounds. As darkness halted the firing that night of January 16, Dull Knife had been given Major Weston's answer to his last stand, now awaited only Maheo's.

When midnight passed with no sign from his god, and the black hours crawled away toward daylight with nothing but the eerie whistle of the winter wind rewarding his lonely vigil, the old chief told his people that it was time for the last prayer—Maheo had abandoned them. But even as those among them who could still move dragged themselves painfully forward for the blessing, Maheo relented. The wind died away and a great stillness fell.

High Bear, the last of the unwounded warriors, raised his head, sniffed the heavy air, grunted the guttural words with sudden hope. *"Zextoeto sanistove!* Snow! Big snow!" he whispered fiercely. "Do you not smell it, father!"

"Aye," answered Dull Knife. "It may be a big one as you say, but it is too late."

"No!" denied High Bear savagely. "Don't say that. It's a sign. Maheo has sent us a sign."

"He has sent us a blanket," muttered the old man dispiritedly, "to cover us when we are dead."

"A blanket will cover many things, father. This one will cover your tracks."

"My tracks, my son?"

"Aye. When the snow starts, you are going out of here. You and all the women and little ones who can still walk. If the storm does not fail you, your tracks will be gone when the sun comes."

"The sun will come but there will be no tracks. We are not going. We will all die together."

"No, father. Those who can walk will go with the snow."

"But *you*," objected Dull Knife. "You do not speak of going yourself, yet you can walk."

High Bear said nothing. Without taking his eyes from the old man, he dropped the muzzle of his rifle and shot himself through the foot. "Those who can walk," he repeated softly, "will go with the snow."

The first flakes fell an hour before daylight. Within seconds, the wind followed them in. Shortly the fall thickened, the wind increased swiftly to gale force. With half an hour of darkness remaining, there were four inches of fresh snow over the old crust and the rising wind was piling Maheo's last-minute blanket deeper with each howling sweep.

The last goodbyes were affectionately said, the tearful embraces silently given and received. Only minutes before daylight, Dull Knife and his little band of unwounded slipped over the edge of the bluff and were gone.

There were nine of them—the old chief, Red Bird's mother, two other squaws, four small children and Red Bird himself. As the warrior of the party and at the parting insistence of High Bear and the other braves, the boy took Little Wolf's treasured Winchester, together with the last four cartridges which would fit it. Dull Knife's heartsick group had no other arms, no food, no blankets. And they were 179 miles from their desperate objective—Pine Ridge and the doubtful sanctuary of the Sioux Agency.

They did not look back as they crept down the narrow defile which gave hidden egress from the blufftops, northward, below and past Meeker's dozing, cold-numbed troops. Behind them, where they lay sharp and black upon the new snow's whiteness, stretching across the open ground between the rifle pit and the head of the escape gully, their tracks were already filling rapidly.

Wyoming's willful climate has been known to make hairy-chested mountain men weep like maiden ladies. And to make red-faced liars out of better weather prophets than High Bear. It will bluster up a blizzard in July, breathe a melting sigh of June warmth in January. Or it will simply call in all bets and sit there doing nothing—as it did with daybreak of that seventeenth.

The snow thinned out the minute it had shielded Dull Knife's withdrawal past Meeker's position, stopped altogether by five-thirty. The wind fell dead at six, having lived just long enough to blow a nice clear hole in the clouds over the Hat Creek bluffs.

Lundy's and Meeker's carbines went to work at six-fifteen. There was no reply from the Cheyenne.

Shortly after sunup the cavalrymen were joined by Jules Stienberg's and Merle Davis's C and D Company riflemen, the

141

infantry having come up during the night and waited, with Weston and Hayes on the flats to the east, for daylight to guide them into G and H Troops' positions. Even Hayes's artillerymen liberated Springfields from the infantry supply train and headed up the slopes to get in on the kill.

Encircling the Hat Creek redoubt of the Cheyenne were nearly three hundred white riflemen. Not an officer or man among them knew at the moment how many Indians were left of Dull Knife's original 151. Lundy's guess, given Weston when the latter worked his way up the southern spur of the bluffs at 8 A.M., was very close. "Not over thirty-five, forty, all told," grunted the taciturn noncom. "With likely no more'n five, six bucks still able to squint acrost a set of sights."

As he said it, Weston looked at him. "Well, I guess this is it." He nodded slowly.

"It is," agreed the other. "You want another rag waved first?"

"Is there any use?"

"It'll look good in your report."

"Go ahead."

"Yes sir. Sam—"

Meeker, who had spent most of the morning running liaison between his company lieutenant on the north bluff and Weston on the flats below, had just come up the south wall with the latter. He winced at Lundy's call. "Here," he answered aloud for official ears. Then, stepping up to Lundy and side-mouthing it for private reference. "You son of a round-heeled squaw! And after all I've did for you!"

"Never mind getting sloppy about it," grinned his benefactor. "I know you're grateful. Tear off a chunk from one of them ammo tarps and take a walk."

"Yes *sir!*" gritted Meeker, seeing Weston moving in, "thank you, *sir!*" He ripped away a yard of the bleached canvas, snagged it on his bayonet, gave Lundy a look that should have fused the crossed sabers on his collar buttons, stepped clear of G Troop's covering boulders and into the open sweep of the blufftop.

He walked out about ten paces, hesitated, waved the faded canvas tentatively.

Of the four Cheyenne shots which answered the gesture, the closest one shattered itself on the haft of his bayonet, breaking the blade's barrel clamp and fluttering Weston's surrender flag into the snow like a wing-hit grouse. Meeker broke off negotiations without awaiting orders. He beat the second round of Indian fire back to the breastworks by a face-first slide and a muddy mouthful of Third Cavalry endearments for Lundy which would have cremated the ears of an artillery mule.

The latter turned at once to Weston. "Well, Major, you convinced?"

"Yes. God forgive us, Lundy. We've no choice now."

"We ain't. How you want it to go?"

"Send Meeker back to Hayes." The artilleryman, ranking Weston's lieutenants, was now in command on the north flank. "Tell him to start in when we do. Advance in skirmish order and keep firing until we're into them." He paused, shaking his head, his sensitive mouth tightly clamped. "We'll be as quick as we can about it, Lundy. It ought not to take more than ten minutes, should it?"

"More likely five, sir." He turned to the unhappy Meeker, unable, even in a moment whose tragedy was clearer to him than to any white man on the Hat Creek bluffs, to suppress his hardbitten pleasure. It was the first time in twenty years that he had outranked his old friend. A man could be forgiven for rubbing it into the feisty little rooster. "All right, Sergeant!" he braced him, "don't just scrunch up there holding on to your water. You heard the Major. On your horse!"

Meeker had not yet gotten up from his dive into the breastwork boulders. He did not bother to now. Saluting from the ground, he growled something for Lundy's tender benefit, slid over the edge of the bluff, rolled down its precipitous slope toward his tethered mount.

Three minutes later Weston, watching the north bluff command post through his glasses, saw him pile off his lathered horse and salute Hayes. The next moment Hayes was waving the acknowledgment into the glasses and Weston was returning the signal. He gave the artilleryman sixty seconds to relay the order down his lines, then moved his own men out. There were no brave bugles blaring, no bright regimental guidons flying, no dramatic "forward ho!" to spur the glorious charge. He merely turned to the troops nearest him and called quietly, "All right, men, let's move in."

The ring of white rifle steel shrunk in on the Cheyenne position in a matter of seconds, its 270-odd barrels snarling in the terrifyingly deliberate cadence of aimed, timed fire. The four

143

hostile rifles spat thinly, fell silent at once. Not a trooper was hit. There was no return fire after the first fifty yards of the advance.

At yard-200, with less than forty paces remaining, Weston faltered, shouted to the troops to halt and take knee rests. When the last Springfield was shouldered, he ordered Lundy forward to offer a final surrender chance in Cheyenne. Knowing it was useless, the latter saluted and started in.

There was no fear now, but only a deep pity in the giant Oklahoman's heart. Long arms upraised, palms held flatly outward, he walked ahead. He was less than ten yards from the Cheyenne when he halted and called out to them. As his deep voice broke across the mounting stillness, three Indians staggered up out of the shallow pit. One had a split-handled camp axe, one an empty rifle clubbed by the barrel, the third a rusted Fort Robinson butcher knife. From the throats of all three, while the startled white troops held their fire, unbidden, now came the last wolf howl of the Cheyenne war cry. With it, the three survivors stumbled toward the waiting rifles.

The pointblank blast of a hundred shots ripped into them. They were torn bodily apart and were dead before the echo of their hoarse defiance died away in the Wyoming hills.

Of the three, one lived long enough to totter within a few feet of the motionless Lundy. The stricken Indian came to a stop, riddled by a score of body shots. In the little instant of suspended time before it happened, Lundy's eyes widened. Even as they did, the dying Cheyenne held the rusted knife in both hands, plunged it to its bloody hilt into her own body.

The third and last of the Powder River Cheyenne to die on the barren plateau of the Hat Creek bluffs was a squaw.

Wild Hog's woman had lived out her dark prophecy and the Dull Knife Raid was over.

Weston stood at the south rim of the tiny crater which had housed the Cheyenne's final stand. It was a natural, shallow amphitheater in the bluff's top, perhaps a dozen paces in diameter, four or five deet deep. In it were twenty-eight emaciated bodies; all that remained of a once feared and powerful people.

But were they all?

The only unbroken snow on the blufftop lay opposite Weston, across the crater. It had been protected from the converging trample of trooper boots by a narrow gully which headed just north of the death pit and, deepening swiftly, angled down to the east to exit on the flatlands below. There its mouth was apparently impassable and was, in fact, so choked with giant boulders and slide rock that none of the white command had thought of it as a possible passage to the blufftop. The upper gully had lain in full view of the troops the afternoon before, but its lower course had been blocked off by irregularities in the blufftop between the Cheyenne position and both Meeker's men on the north and Lundy's on the south. In the certainty of the entrapment it had not occurred to any of the attacking force that the tortuous declivity presented a potential escape route for the cornered Cheyenne. Even had the thought occurred, it would have been dismissed. Until broad daylight the flatlands below, including the defile's boulder-jammed opening, had been sealed off by Weston's main camp. And after daylight, a packrat could not have gotten into the gully without being seen by Lundy's and Meeker's entrenched riflemen.

The possibility that the Cheyenne might have used the route to flee the bluff still was not apparent to the white command—for a very obvious reason. It was this reason which Weston and his staff now studied. And thought so little of.

The distance from the Cheyenne rifle pit to the heading of the gully was not over thirty feet. A hundred pairs of white eyes had seen that clear line of half-filled moccasin tracks stretching across its untrampled snows and, seeing them, shrugged and looked away. A Fort Lincoln rawtail could unravel that line of hostile footprints. It was that simple. Its turned-in Indian toe marks pointed *from* the gully *toward* the pit. Obviously, and despite its choked lower opening, a few of the Cheyenne had used the gully to gain the blufftop. That was all. There was no more to it.

Weston, on the point of shrugging off the tracks like the others, turned to find Lundy at his side. The big sergeant kept his voice down, hunched his shoulder in the direction of the gully. "Major, let's mosey over yonder a minute. Down that draw just a piece. I got something to show you."

As they started off, Hayes and two of the young lieutenants broke off their inspection of the pit to tag along. Lundy glanced back, scowling uneasily. "We ain't going to need no staffwork on this, Major. Best give the boys something else to do." Weston looked at him questioningly, took note of his scowl, accepted its warning, waved at once to Hayes. "Martin,

145

I think we'd best be getting under way. Take over, please. We won't be a minute."

Hayes held up, passed the order along. There was no dissent. Weston's youthful staff had already had more than it needed of the Hat Creek post-mortem. Gladly enough, its members turned back to the work of falling-in their companies preparatory to leaving the bluff.

Lundy purposely led the way along the Cheyenne tracks, making sure his and Weston's footsteps overlay and confused those of the Indians. Ten yards into the gully and out of sight of the gathering troops above, he halted and pointed ahead. In the undisturbed crust of the wind-sheltered snow, the moccasin prints of the Cheyenne lay etched in glass-sharp relief. Weston's brow furrowed as he studied them. Lundy said nothing, stood waiting tensely for his companion to get the Indian point.

Slowly Weston's eyes widened. "Good Lord!" he muttered, half aloud and to himself, and, having muttered it, stared in continued silence along the narrow track.

"Yeah," said Lundy, low voiced. "They walked backwards till they got into the gully. Oldest Injun trick in the world. Raynald and them Sioux slit-eyes of his would have spotted it in a minute. The way it is, it's only between me and you, Major—*and him.*"

"Him?"

"Dull Knife. He ain't among them back yonder."

"No?"

"No sir. We know he was with them when they made this bluff yesterday. As far as our boys from the post are concerned, he could be any one of them bucks back there in the pit. They're all of them so froze black and bad shot up you cain't tell one from the other. But as far as you and me go, he ain't back there. I'll guarantee that, Major."

"Are you *certain,* man?"

"I'd know that fierce-proud old devil anywhere short of hell and shriveled to a cinder."

"All right, Lundy—where does it leave us?"

"I make it out this way. There's nine of them in the bunch that got away. One growed man, three squaws, four little kids, one bigger one. They ain't been gone two hours. Say they've made seven, eight miles at the outside. They're weak and sick and starved crazy. The prairie's wide open past this stretch of Hat Creek brush."

146

"And?"

"They're ours if we want 'em."

Weston did not answer for so long that Lundy began to get edgy. Somebody was bound to follow down from above any second. Here and now was no time to be standing there staring off into nothing. He cleared his throat, moved quickly forward. "Well, Major, yonder's your last chance. There ain't but one question to answer now. *What do you want did about them tracks?*"

Weston came around slowly. His forehead contracted as though with conscious effort to bring his mind back from a long, tortured look into nowhere. Then, the frown lines were gone, leaving his lean face at last at rest, his gentle gray eyes quiet and untroubled.

"What tracks, Lundy?" he asked softly, and turned and walked up out of the gully.

CHAPTER 25

THE SHALLOW EARTH atop the Hat Creek bluffs was frozen as hard as the Wyoming limestone which underlay it. No attempt was made to bury the Cheyenne dead. Nameless, they were left uncovered where they lay. The troops were formed up and marching within the hour. They camped early that afternoon, were under way once more with daybreak of the 18th.

Leaving the column under Hayes, Weston pushed ahead accompanied by Lundy and Meeker. They made a brief noon halt to boil coffee and grain the horses.

While Meeker laid the fire and broke out the nosebags Lundy, never at rest in Indian country, climbed the nearest rise to scout the way ahead. He was back before the snow in Meeker's mess pan had begun to melt. "We got company," he told Weston tersely. "Best part of a full troop of horse heading in for our smoke."

"Jackson?" asked the latter nervously, the name which had been growing in his mind all morning popping out automatically.

"Nope, these ain't any of our boys. They're angling up from near straightaway south. Most likely some of the General's lads from down Laramie way. We'll see soon enough. Yonder comes the 'bad news now."

He broke off to nod toward the southern spur of the rise, not missing the grimness which tightened his companion's mouth corners at the mention of Crook, and understanding it. He waited beside the slender C.O. while the approaching officer slid his horse down the ridge and brought him to a snow-showering halt in front of them.

"Major Weston?"

"Right."

"Lieutenant Foreman, sir. Headquarters Company, Fort Laramie." The youth dropped his salute, smiled a little stiffly. "Looks like we're too late for the fun, I'm afraid."

"A little, Lieutenant. My column is following us half a day back. It's all over, sir."

In response to the youngster's natural interest, he compressed the week's action into less than twenty words, concluded with a question of his own. One which brought the chance meeting to short order and closed it with the same brevity. "Did you get to talk to General Crook before you left Laramie, Lieutenant?"

"No sir. I was out on patrol when Captain Jackson reported in from Robinson. When I got in, the General's orders to head north on scout were waiting. I just picked up field rations and pulled out again."

"I see." Watching him, Lundy saw Weston's gray eyes darken, and that was all. "When did the Captain's report reach Laramie, sir?"

"Nearly a week ago. I believe it was the 10th or the 11th. I'm really not sure which."

"I am," said Weston cryptically.

"Yeah," added Lundy bitterly. "Me too. He was with us on the 10th. Make it the 11th, Lieutenant. And then add five minutes."

"Five minutes, Sergeant?" frowned the young officer, eyeing him sharply. "What for?"

"For him to pile off his damn horse and leg it for the telegraph shack. The lousy little colonel-kissing son of a—"

"That will do, Lundy." Weston cut him off without rebuke. "Well, Lieutenant, I guess you can't tell us anything then.
148

Naturally, I've been wondering about the General's reaction to all this."

"Yes sir, naturally. But I *can* tell you one thing, Major."

"Yes."

"You won't have to wonder much longer."

"So? How's that, Lieutenant?"

"General Crook is waiting for you at Fort Robinson."

Crook, in his patient, kindly way, made it as easy for him as any general officer in his position could have. He received him in Weston's office, ordered the outer office cleared, instructed Ferris to admit no one, even sent his own orderly out of the room. When the door had closed behind the latter, he laid it out in four-letter words for the Robinson C.O. He spoke clearly and quickly, in that straight way one honorable man will take with another. Keeping it mercifully uncolored, he reviewed his listener's palpable failures at Robinson, concluded with the earnest hope that he would understand what he, Crook, now had regretfully to tell him.

In the following stillness, Howell Weston took a last, slow look through his favorite parade ground window. When he had finished it, he squared his thin shoulders, came around and to attention.

"Yes sir," he said quietly.

"You are relieved of rank and command—will report back to Sheridan at Fort Lincoln on or before February first. Jackson takes over here. I'm sorry, Weston."

Weston saluted, saying nothing.

Crook's pale eyes softened.

"You did your best, sir. We both know that."

"*I wonder,*" said Howell Weston softly. And went out and through the outer office.

He did not look back.

He left at six the next morning, while the sergeants were barking out roll call on the parade ground and the post was in its most deserted hour.

He had said his few personal goodbyes the previous evening—to Meeker, Lundy, Amy Lohburg, her bright-eyed children—to a handful of embarrassed troopers, headed by Corporal Peter Feeney, who had come to shake his hand and to stammer their awkward respects.

Amy had been the hardest. When she had told him about

149

Lundy and herself, he had necessarily answered with the usual formalities. The big hillman would make a good mate for the gaunt prairie woman; a devoted and patient father for young Billy and the girls. Still, a man had to know his own heart. And be honest with it. In that last difficult minute, facing her in the soft fall of the parlor lamplight, Howell Weston had known what had been unadmittedly growing in his heart for Amy Lohburg. And had known, too, from the long, slow way she had taken his hand and held his eyes with hers, that she shared the knowledge and meant for him to understand that she did.

But now all that was behind. Ahead lay only the frozen slush of the company street and its ending at the main gates. On a borrowed troop horse, looking neither right nor left, Weston rode his lonely way out of Fort Robinson.

The remaining farewells were painful, wordless things, accidents only of his mount's route and the day's beginning routine.

Major John Tenney Jackson, new oak leaves agleam in the morning sun, stepped out of the C.O.'s office on his way to breakfast. He stopped and drew himself up. Lieutenant Frank Ferris, coming out behind him, heard the brittle chop of the horse's hoofs. He looked up, flushed guiltily, added his stiff salute to Jackson's. Weston rode past, turned the far corner of the headquarters building, was gone.

"Poor devil," grimaced Jackson. "You can't help feeling sorry for him. Too bad. Just no real guts—"

Past the farrier's shed and the quartermaster's depot, turning past the guardhouse for the main gates, Weston sat his mount in continued, eyes-ahead silence. From the iron-barred grating of Cell 17, an expressionless red face watched him approach. *"Eneamen,* my brothers," called Left Hand, "come and see who passes by."

Wild Hog and Lone Crow dragged themselves to his side, gritting their teeth against the pain of their unhealed wounds. The jangling scrape of their leg irons jarred the morning stillness, carried clearly to Weston. He checked his mount, turned in the saddle, peered uncertainly at the guardhouse. He saw them, then, and swung his horse full toward them. He raised his left hand, fingertips to forehead, saluted them gravely. Without hesitation, the three Cheyenne returned the gesture of parting, deep respect.

"He never lied to us," said Lone Crow to his companions.

"He sits tall on that pony," answered Left Hand soberly.

"Enitoeme, Evoxpohess!" Wild Hog called the Cheyenne courage-word suddenly and impulsively to the waiting white officer. Then, proudly, in his halting English and once more touching his fingers to his forehead, *"We salute you, White Hair!"*

Weston did not answer as he turned his horse, but the Indians understood that. They had seen the look on his face and the way he sat a little straighter in the saddle when he went away.

Lundy had the main gate guard detail. He was gold-bricking it with the off-duty Meeker in the warmth of the coming sun behind the sentry box when the guard-corporal's warning broke sharply. "Brass ho, Sarge! Look alive!"

He peered around the corner of the box, pulled his head back. "It's him," he said to Meeker.

The two sergeants stepped to the edge of the wagon road, hit their braces and held them properly. As Weston passed, they snapped their salutes, eyes dead ahead and not looking at him. He checked the horse. Only when their eyes broke, shifting to met his, did he return the salute. Then he did it quickly and rode on. Meeker and Lundy exchanged startled looks. A man could not be sure—he had moved on so fast and sharp—but both old soldiers would have sworn that as he turned away, Captain Howell Weston was smiling!

They watched him now, as he put his horse up the long rise of the military wagon road east of the post. And watched him still, as he pulled the animal in at the top of the grade and sat him uncertainly, as though looking back for the last time upon Fort Robinson and his final failure. Then they saw his shoulders go back and his head come up. He sat that way, straight and proud against the morning sun, for an endless moment. Then he swung his horse and was gone.

Meeker shook his head, turned to his grim-faced companion. "Now what the hell do you suppose that damn grin was all about?" he frowned, breaking the long silence with the puzzled reference to Weston's strange look as he had turned away from them. "I'd give a week's pay to find out."

"Save your money," grunted Lundy. "I *know* what it was all about."

"Yeah?"

"Yeah."

Lundy fell silent, looking far away and across the windswept crest of the distant rise. At last, and slowly, he turned back to Meeker.

"He was a better man than Jackson," he said softly. *"And he knew it."*

In the Fort Robinson sawmill, upon Weston's return from the Hat Creek bluffs, "hauled in by the wagonload and stacked like cordwood," lay the frozen bodies of sixty-four Cheyenne. In the week of his commander's absence from the post, Jackson's mopping-up operation, augmented by Crook's relief patrols advancing from Fort Laramie, captured and brought in an additional sixty-five of the fugitives who had been bypassed in the first night's drive beyond the White River crossing. Of the remaining twenty-two of the original one hundred and fifty-one prisoners in B barracks that dark sunset of January 9, 1879, ten were never found and were presumed dead, nine had been allowed to escape at Hat Creek, three were in irons in the post guardhouse.

All the surviving Cheyenne, with the exception of "twenty troublemakers" who were sent back to Darlington, were transferred to Pine Ridge and allowed to "stay north." There is still in existence an excellent photo of the "troublemakers" taken on their way south. Identified, are Blacksmith, Wild Hog, Tangled Hair, Porcupine, Old Man and those inseparable old murderers, Left Hand and Lone Crow. The caption reads, "taken at Dodge City, Kansas—with their white friends." It may be assumed that the caption was not written by an Indian.

General George Crook, putting his official postscript to the tragedy, wrote in anger and sorrow to the White Father in Washington; "Among these Cheyenne were some of the bravest and most efficient of the auxiliaries who acted under General Mackenzie and myself in the campaign against the hostile Sioux in 1876 and 1877. I still preserve a grateful remembrance of their distinguished services, which the government seems to have forgotten."

Dull Knife and his little band reached Pine Ridge after eighteen days of blizzard-driven flight. Red Bird survived to become the latter-day head of the Northern Cheyenne. The old chief, his grandfather, died in 1883. He was buried on Big Butte, overlooking the Rosebud River, along which he had served so faithfully with his old friend, Three Stars.

Little Wolf, that "crafty red war monger" and indomitable distruster of the white brother, doubled back into the

Sand Hills below Fort Robinson following his separation from Dull Knife, and lived the entire winter "fat and easy" on antelope and buffalo "within a day's march of the biggest post of Pony Soldiers west of Fort Lincoln." He surrendered quietly and with the full honors of war to Lieutenant W. P. Clark (the famed "White Hat" Clark who engineered the coming-in of Crazy Horse) the following spring, and was given a fine new reservation along the Tongue River in southeastern Montana.

Here, he lived for thirty years before his death in 1909. At the end he was a very old man, totally blind and nearly helpless but as much the proud, unconquered War Chief as upon that long-gone night beside the Clear Fork when he faced the wavering Council of Elders and delivered his bitter valedictory.

"Remember what I say, my brothers. Peace is never put into the laps of beggars. It is seized only by the hands of warriors."

Truly, when he had said that, Hokom-xaaxceta, the last War Chief of the Powder River Cheyenne, had said it all.

Nohetto.

After that, there was no more.

ABOUT THE AUTHOR

WILL HENRY was born and grew up in Missouri, where he attended Kansas City Junior College. Upon leaving school, he lived and worked throughout the Western states, acquiring the background of personal experience reflected later in the realism of his books. Currently residing in California, he writes for motion pictures, as well as continuing his research into frontier lore and legend, which are the basis for his unique blend of history and fiction. Ten of his novels have been purchased for motion picture production, and several have won top literary awards, including the Wrangler trophy of the National Cowboy Hall of Fame, the first Levi Strauss Golden Saddleman and five Western Writers of America Spurs. Mr. Henry is a recognized authority on America's frontier past, particularly that relating to the American horseback Indian of the High Plains. His books include *Chiricahua*; *No Survivors*; *I, Tom Horn*; *From Where the Sun Now Stands*; and *The Squaw Killers*.